W9-AYP-644

DISCARD

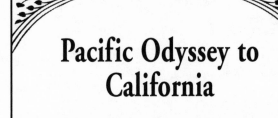

Pacific Odyssey to
California

1905

Books by Laurie Lawlor

The Worm Club
How to Survive Third Grade
Addie Across the Prairie
Addie's Long Summer
Addie's Dakota Winter
George on His Own
Gold in the Hills
Little Women *(a movie novelization)*

Heartland series
Heartland: Come Away with Me
Heartland: Take to the Sky
Heartland: Luck Follows Me

American Sisters series
West Along the Wagon Road 1852
A *Titanic* Journey Across the Sea 1912
Voyage to a Free Land 1630
Adventure on the Wilderness Road 1775
Crossing the Colorado Rockies 1864
Down the Río Grande 1829
Horseback on the Boston Post Road 1704
Exploring the Chicago World's Fair 1893
Pacific Odyssey to California 1905

American SISTERS
Pacific Odyssey to California
1905

Laurie Lawlor

A MINSTREL® HARDCOVER
PUBLISHED BY POCKET BOOKS

New York   London   Toronto   Sydney   Singapore

A MINSTREL HARDCOVER

 A Minstrel Book published by
POCKET BOOKS, a division of Simon & Schuster, Inc.
1230 Avenue of the Americas, New York, NY 10020

ISBN: 0-671-03925-3

First Minstrel Books hardcover printing July 2001

10   9   8   7   6   5   4   3   2   1

A MINSTREL BOOK and colophon are registered trademarks
of Simon & Schuster, Inc.

Cover illustration by Kam Mak

Printed in the U.S.A.

For Thich Nhat Hanh,

poet and teacher

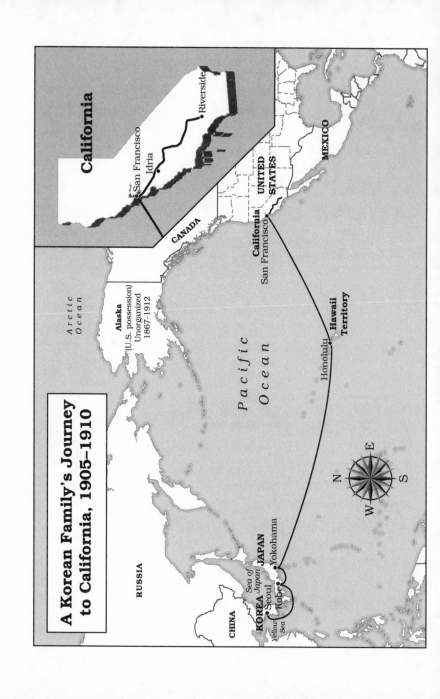

A Korean Family's Journey to California, 1905–1910

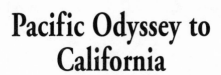

Pacific Odyssey to California

1905

Introduction

The story of America is the story of a nation of immigrants. From all over the world men, women, and children have come to the United States to find a new beginning.

Pacific Odyssey tells the little-told story of a group of immigrants to the West who have mostly been neglected or overlooked by history textbooks. Between 1849, the beginning of the California gold rush, and 1924, the year the Immigration Act was passed specifically barring their entry, nearly one million Asians crossed the Pacific Ocean to build new lives in the United States.

Thousands of Asians worked in western mines or helped build the transcontinental railroad. They took low-paying construction jobs in western towns and cities. They performed back-breaking field work that helped transform irrigated deserts into fertile fruit-growing regions. Many white landowners, railroad barons, and mining moguls viewed Asian labor as cheap and the lives of these people as dispensable. In Hawaii, where this book begins, sugarcane plantation owners purposefully pitted different Asian groups against one another in an effort to break strikes and lower overall wages.

One hundred years ago in California and elsewhere in the West, the concept of the "yellow peril" was promoted in books, newspapers, magazines, plays, posters, and political speeches. The "yellow peril" concept was based on the racist idea that whites were inherently superior to Chinese, Japanese, and Koreans, who were viewed as dangerous and potentially damaging to the American economy and American ideals. Beneath this widespread prejudice was economic self-interest. Asian immigrants worked hard for less money. Some Americans accused them of taking jobs away from white workers.

In many western towns and cities, Asian children were not allowed to go to school with white children. They were refused service in white-owned restaurants, barbershops, and public recreational facilities. Some white landlords refused to rent them houses or lease them land. In 1913 the California legislature passed laws that essentially banned Asian-born immigrants from owning land. Even when they were educated, many Asian immigrants continued to face prejudice and dead-end jobs. Worse yet, until 1952,

Asian immigrants and other people "of color" newly arrived from Japan, China, and Korea were denied naturalized citizenship, a prerequisite to vote.

Like other Asian immigrants, Koreans were treated as second-class citizens. Between 1903 and 1920, a total of nearly eight thousand men, women, and children fled poverty, famine, drought, and political oppression in Korea and sailed to the United States to better themselves and their families. Many hoped to return one day to their native land. Like Chinese and Japanese immigrants, the Koreans were mostly young. More than ninety percent were between the ages of sixteen and forty-five. They were farmers, city laborers, government clerks, students, miners, police officers, and teachers. Nearly seventy percent could read. Many had been encouraged to come to the United States by American missionaries in Korea. Nearly forty percent had converted to Christianity before they crossed the Pacific.

In 1910, when Japan took over Korea, first generation Korean immigrants faced a crisis. They could not go back to their country. Korean language, government, religion, schools, and laws had been forcibly changed. For many, the shift from "sojourner" to settler was difficult and heart-wrenching. *Pacific Odyssey* examines the struggle of one Korean immigrant family, "strangers from a strange shore," who were forced to create a life in a new, often hostile country.

Prologue

1910

It is nearly dusk, the last hours of light. Two girls
stand beneath a secret pine tree and watch the shadows shift against the hills that smell of wind and dust
and juniper. The valley below darkens as if filling with
black water. Above loom deep purple mountains not
so different from the rocky peaks of the mountains in
the girls' birthplace, a country they can barely remember. *Choson*, Land of Morning Calm.

"What if she doesn't come?"

"Quiet. This is her favorite place. She'll be here this
time, I'm sure."

A breeze twists the strips of colorful cloth the girls
tied to the branches to appease mountain spirits. Now
the wind bends the tops of trees and makes a sound

like water rushing, like waves remembered from their trip across the ocean long, long ago. The girls shiver. So much has happened since then.

They wait with an air of quiet expectancy, shifting from one foot to the other like patient deer. This is the third evening they have come. To be disappointed again will be too much to bear. They both know this, though they don't say it aloud. Father's words, part thunder, part salt, still ring in their ears: "Do not speak your sister's name again."

What use is there to offer forgiveness when there is no one to forgive?

The elder girl sighs. "Night's coming."

"Mother and Father will wonder where we've gone," the other replies.

And yet the two sisters linger a moment longer. Then another. Afraid to admit what they both fear most.

Maybe we have lost her forever.

Chapter 1

Oahu, Hawaii

1905

Jae-Mi held tight to the rope swing and leaned back as far as she could. Everything that spring morning in 1905 seemed to tumble upside-down. Blue ocean and blue sky traded places. *Sky-ocean. Sky-ocean. Sky-ocean.* The eight-year-old didn't care that the soiled hem of her *han-bok* dress flew up over her knees in a forbidden, unlady-like fashion. She didn't care that the tips of her long black braids brushed the dirty deck of the S.S. *Iberia.* She swung back and forth, higher and higher. The knot-ted rope squeaked against the overhead pipe and sang:

Kae-guk chinch-wi
Kae-guk chinch-wi

Jae-Mi cocked her head to one side. "Hear that?"

Eleven-year-old Su-Na gave her sister another vigorous push. "What?"

"*Kae-guk chinch-wi.* 'The country is open, go forward.' The same thing the men shouted to each other when we left Korea. What does it mean?"

"'America is vast, do not be afraid.'"

Jae-Mi pumped harder. How pleasing to think that a swing could give encouragement!

Kae-guk chinch-wi

Kae-guk chinch-wi

Father had told Jae-Mi the day before they left Korea that in Hawaii there was no hunger or fear, sadness or suffering. This island paradise was part of America, he said.

"Is America an island?" Jae-Mi asked.

"No," Father said, and laughed. "It would take many years to walk across America. America is a huge country, huge and free, where everyone is equal."

Kae-guk chinch-wi

Kae-guk chinch-wi

Jae-Mi scanned the endless horizon. If America was so open, vast, and big, why couldn't she see it? She wished they were going directly to America, not Hawaii. Hawaii sounded too much like the heaven that the missionaries always talked about. She didn't know if she wanted to go to a place where there were lots of dead people and angels floating around with wings. Jae-Mi leaned back and pointed her toes. "Su-Na, what is a free country where everyone is equal?"

Su-Na shrugged. "I don't know." She gave her sister another push. "All I know is that we are not staying forever and I'm glad. As soon as Father's rich, we're going home again."

"You will be very, very old by the time you cross America."

Su-Na scowled. "What are you talking about?"

"It will take years and years and years and years."

"We are going to see Grandmother and Grandfather again very soon," Su-Na insisted. "Father promised. We are sojourners, he said, not settlers. We have to go back. We left everything behind, except our clothes, some bedding —"

Kae-guk chinch-wi
Kae-guk chinch-wi

"What is a sojourner?" Jai-Mi demanded.

"Someone who visits for a little while."

"Hawaii is far away for such a little-while visit. Perhaps Father will change his mind."

Su-Na puffed out her cheeks in frustration. She let out a great breath of air. What did her stupid sister know?

"If I had wings like an angel," Jae-Mi boasted, "I would be in America by now."

"My turn!" interrupted Hi-Jong. Their seven-year-old sister charged toward them across the deck. Small and thin, Hi-Jong had dark, measuring eyes that always watched to see how rice cakes and affection were divided. "Get off my swing."

Jae-Mi pretended she couldn't hear Hi-Jong. Back home Jae-Mi could swing the highest in the swinging contests with the other girls. Here on the boat there wasn't room for her to stand up and swing. She had to sit. Even so, she liked to imagine a whole mob of people watching her and cheering.

"Stop!" demanded Hi-Jong. She quivered with rage. Why did Jae-Mi think that she could keep the swing that was made for *her* by the *chong gak*, the bachelor neighbors, who were going with them to Hawaii? Hi-Jong and her sisters called them Uncle and Second Uncle out of respect. Swinging in the fresh breeze, the Uncles said, would cure Hi-Jong of her seasickness. They called her Pretty Little Flower and gave her candy made from honey and pine nuts. And now Jae-Mi, who was clumsy and oafish and ugly, was spoiling everything. Why was Su-Na allowing such injustice? "Get off my swing!"

Jae-Mi only laughed and kicked out her feet. She tilted backward. *Sky-ocean. Sky-ocean. Sky-ocean.* Upside down, her sister's frown looked like a grotesque smile. "'The country is open, go forward!'" she taunted and swung out of Hi-Jong's reach again. The horizon stretched on and on until Jae-Mi felt dizzy and had to gulp for air.

Hi-Jong howled. The sound was horrible and familiar. In an instant, Jae-Mi's wonderful flight ended. The swing wobbled and twisted so that her legs swung round and everything spun and lurched the way she remembered it on the first days aboard the ship when everyone was seasick.

"*O, wa!*" hissed Su-Na, who held tight to the rope. "Don't be selfish. Must you always disturb good *ki-bun?* If Father finds out about this disharmony he will leave the bedside of our poor, sick mother and come up here to punish you."

Jai-Mi did not flinch even though the skin on her arm stung. She wriggled free from Su-Na's pincer grip and jumped off the swing. Stubbornly she refused to let go of the rope so Hi-Jong could not climb on and enjoy her victory.

"Give her the swing!" Su-Na demanded, louder than she meant to. She looked over her shoulder to make sure that no one was near enough to hear this outburst, which might certainly invite bad spirits. How many times had Mother told her that women were to be seen and not heard? Even in the middle of the Pacific Ocean, miles and miles from home, someone might be watching. Someone might scold her and remind her that she was nothing but a worthless girl. "It's Hi-Jong's turn," Su-Na said quietly and gave Jae-Mi a sharp tug.

Jae-Mi's fist clenched the rough rope tighter. She

looked at her whimpering sister. Hi-Jong's *nun-mul* did not impress her in the least. She was always sobbing. "Here," Su-Na growled, "take it, *nun-mul* baby." She shoved the rope in her sister's direction.

"Apologize," Su-Na insisted.

Jae-Mi's mouth hardened into a line.

"Apologize," Su-Na repeated. She had to make sure proper *ki-bun* was restored. This was a woman's duty, she knew.

Jae-Mi made a short, halfhearted bow. "Sorry," she murmured.

Hi-Jong smiled, victorious. She quickly climbed onto the swing. "Push me," she commanded.

Now it was Jae-Mi's turn to push. She gave Hi-Jong a tremendous shove that sent her sailing. She had meant the push to terrify Hi-Jong. Instead Hi-Jong squealed with delight. "Higher!" she shouted.

Jae-Mi pushed again. Hi-Jong laughed.

"Can you see Korea?" Jae-Mi demanded.

Hi-Jong shook her head.

"Can you see Hawaii?" Jae-Mi called. "Better still, can you see America?"

Hi-Jong shook her head again. "Higher."

"Careful," Su-Na warned. She did not trust Jae-Mi's enthusiasm. Whenever her sisters came together, they were soon arguing or fighting. Why did they always have to act so disagreeable? Su-Na sighed and leaned against the wall. The entire voyage Mother had been ill and unable to leave her berth. The two girls had been Su-Na's responsibility. She had to keep her eye on her sisters every minute and make sure they stayed out of mischief.

For the past ten days most of the passengers had been seasick. The trip from Korea across the Yellow Sea to Japan had been especially rough. The boat rolled violently and tossed everything from side to side. When they got to Kobe and disembarked, they had to have a second physical exam. Mother was so sick she confessed she was afraid she'd be sent back. But all the men in the uniforms did was peer into the family's ears and eyes and direct them to another, even bigger American steamer.

The S.S. *Iberia* was a huge American ship with two smokestacks and five levels connected by a bewildering maze of stairs. Meals were served belowdeck in a dining hall filled with long tables and benches. For supper there was rice and vegetables and *kimchee*, traditional spicy pickled cabbage and radishes. Su-Na and her family traveled, spoke, and ate exclusively with other Koreans. They shared sleeping quarters with other Koreans. Even the smells were familiar: a piquant wreath of crushed garlic, seaweed, and red chili pepper floated everywhere.

Although this was Su-Na's first trip away from her native city of Seoul, everyone she met aboard the S.S. *Iberia* reminded her of some neighbor back home.

Certainly the people in Hawaii would speak, eat, and dress in the Korean manner, too. And if America was as vast as everyone said, there must be plenty of Koreans there as well. *I'll never have to learn English or learn American ways. Why bother? We'll be returning home soon. After all, we are sojourners.*

So-jour-ners. So-jour-ners. Su-Na said this word over and over to herself in time to the squeaking swing.

Kae-guk chinch-wi
Kae-guk chinch-wi

Hi-Jong swung faster and faster, kicking her feet high into the air. "It is never cold or snowy in Hawaii. And fine colorful clothing grows on trees." There was nothing she could imagine more splendid than a pair of crimson quilted shoes.

"What kind of clothing?" Jae-Mi demanded mischievously. "What if there are only trousers? You will look like a boy."

Hi-Jong ignored her sister's ridiculous statement. Girls never looked like boys. "Father said. He knows everything. Isn't that true, Su-Na?"

Su-Na nodded. Earlier on their voyage, when they landed at Yokohama, she had spotted strangers wearing long dresses that came nearly to their ankles. They wore odd, forked socks. And when she asked Father who these men were, he angrily muttered, "Dwarfish Villains." She was too afraid to ask him what he meant.

"Of course," Su-Na told her sisters, "Father will not allow us to wear the clothes of dwarfish villains."

"Certainly not!" Hi-Jong said, and laughed.

"I should like to look like a dwarfish villain," Jae-Mi announced. "What is a dwarfish villain?"

"A dwarfish villain is not Korean," Su-Na answered in a very wise voice. Her sisters nodded solemnly as if this made perfect sense.

The ocean glinted and galloped. The sunlight on the water danced. "The water is not so dark now," Jae-Mi said, and pointed. And it was true. The deep sea had turned a brilliant green-blue.

Hi-Jong swung slower and slower with no one pushing her. Jae-Mi and Su-Na stared out over the water that seemed to go on forever. "See, the big gray birds are gone," Su-Na said. Hi-Jong dragged her feet, stopped herself, and joined them at the railing. They looked out over the water and noticed small, spry birds skimming the surface.

"They look like spirits," Su-Na said.

"You and your spirits!" Jae-Mi scoffed.

Excitedly, Hi-Jong pointed. "Are those whales?" In the distance floated dark, humpbacked specks.

In the next instant the deck filled with shouting passengers. "Land!"

"There it is! Hawaii!"

Su-Na and her sisters shielded their eyes from the sun and concentrated on a black, dreary spot on the horizon. "How can we fit?" Jae-Mi demanded. "It's no bigger than the tip of my finger." This could not be the green paradise Father had described.

No one else on board seemed disappointed. The Uncles and Second Uncles gathered excitedly to smoke their long pipes and discuss their fabulous futures. The girls bowed, stood at a respectful distance, and listened quietly.

"Just take a breath. You can smell paradise."

"The Chinese call it 'Sandalwood Fragrant Mountain.'"

"What do they know?"

"Imagine. Free housing, medical care, and sixteen dollars a month for a sixty-hour work week. That's nearly sixty-four *won*. I'll have a small fortune in no time. I'll go back home a rich man."

"If you don't gamble all your earnings away."

The Uncles and Second Uncles laughed. They seemed light-hearted now that paradise was so close. In Hawaii life would be splendid. Shiny boxes of black lacquer with brass hinges lined the streets. Along the thoroughfares stood fat bags of rice, packets of seaweed, and good salt fish—all free for the taking. Rolls of cotton and silk cloth hung from trees and fans and fine hats sprouted right out of the ground. All they had to do was lie under a bread tree and coconut palm and eat, drink, and be merry in the cool of the shade, not wanting for anything.

Soon the Uncles were lighting a second and a third pipe and singing old songs about the Dragon Backed Country they had left behind. Their words were filled with longing and their tunes sounded forlorn and lonely.

"Enough!" one Uncle exclaimed. *"He,* tell a funny story." He prodded his neighbor with his elbow. "An amusing America story."

Storyteller Uncle appeared thoughtful for a moment and puffed his pipe. "You have all seen a newfangled bicycle on the streets of Seoul, have you not? In America everyone has his own modern bicycle. The streets are filled with them. Many Americans think that they invented the bicycle. What they don't know is that the go-by-itself wheel was invented in the mountains of China."

The men hissed and spit. "China! We don't want a China story. We want an America story."

Storyteller Uncle smiled and raised a hand to quiet his disturbed audience. "Let me finish. In China the first bicycle had two parts. A 'go-part' and a 'come-back-part.' One day the Chinese fellow who invented the bicycle had a very busy day. He was making repairs, you see. He had to repair the come-back-part. He took this off. Now a curious old woman was walking past his hut. She wanted to know about this strange riding invention. She wanted to try it. So when he wasn't looking, she took the go-part wheel and rode away. On and on, over the countryside she went. She had a fine ride, but when the sun dropped down behind the western mountains, she wanted to go home. But she couldn't because the come-back-part had been taken off. The old woman was never seen again. And that is why the Chinese gave up the dangerous go-by-itself wheel and never became modern like the Americans."

"Fine story!" The Uncles laughed and clapped.

Jae-Mi, too, laughed so that her teeth showed. Su-Na jabbed her hard with her elbow and motioned for her to cover her mouth the way a proper young girl should.

"Do you have another?" one of the Uncles asked. "Tell a Korea story this time."

"Once upon a time there was a thief named Choi," Storyteller Uncle said. "He was well-known among the local villagers for his clever way of getting into houses and his ruthlessness in stealing even from poor people."

The men nodded and shifted on their haunches. They did not need to be told about poverty. Why else had they left Korea? Starvation and want looked them in the eye every morning. Too many years of too many droughts, too many famines. They were accustomed to the Spring Suffering, when there was little rice left in the storerooms and the new rice was still only green shoots. They knew what it was like when there was nothing in the garden and no coins in the cash box to buy rice. But now that the Japanese soldiers were everywhere, food was even more scarce and Spring Suffering lasted all year.

"One night Thief Choi quietly unlocked a family's wooden gate," Storyteller Uncle continued. "He entered the house. In one corner of the bedroom the husband was sound asleep with his wife next to him. In the other corner Thief Choi saw the three children sleeping. All daughters."

One of the Uncles clucked his tongue and shook his head. "Bad omen."

"'What a poor man with three daughters!' Thief Choi said to himself," Storyteller Uncle said. "He felt sorry for the man. So sorry he stepped out of the house as quietly as he had come. He walked away and did not take anything."

The Uncles and Second Uncles smiled and rubbed their hands together. Even a thief pitied a poor man cursed to live out his life without a son.

Su-Na stared at her hands and squirmed uncomfortably. Her wonderful mood was gone and she did not know why. She had heard this story before, but this was the first time she wondered if the tale was about her and her sisters. Once, after Hi-Jong was born, Su-Na heard Mother beg Mrs. Ban-Ja Paik, who had five sons, to sew a few stitches on a new blanket. Soon after that Mother had a baby boy, but he died before his first birthday. When she tried again to have a new blanket stitched by Mrs. Ban-Ja Paik, the next baby was also a boy, but he lived only a week.

Not having any sons made Mother very sad. Secretly, Su-Na hoped that perhaps in Hawaii, where life was perfect, there might be some baby boys available. If brand-new clothing grew on trees, why not brand-new baby boys? Perhaps she and her sisters might find a healthy brother under a palm tree leaf and bring him home to Mother to cheer her spirits. Of course, Father would be very pleased, too. He said he always wanted a son—

"How far away is Korea now?" Jae-Mi's shrill voice jolted Su-Na out of her daydream.

"Too far to go back," Su-Na replied.

Without warning, Hi-Jong began to whimper.

"Not more *nun-mul!*" Jae-Mi said with disgust.

Hi-Jong only cried louder. Life seemed unbearably unpredictable. There was no telling when anything was going to happen. One minute she and her family were in Korea; the next they were traveling far, far away across a dangerous, deep ocean. Grown-ups decided everything. "I have lost it," Hi-Jong said, and sniffed.

"What?" Jae-Mi asked.

"Grandfather's voice."

Su-Na wiped her sister's troubled face with the edge of her *han-bok* sleeve. "You mean you have misplaced the memory?"

Hi-Jong nodded.

"Maybe you did not lose it. Maybe Thief Choi stole it," Jae-Mi said, chuckling.

Su-Na jabbed Jae-Mi with her elbow. "When we get to Hawaii, you'll remember," Su-Na said in a reassuring voice. "No one is confused or unhappy in Hawaii."

"That's because they live in paradise," Jae-Mi added with authority. "Everyone is free and equal. And every day they eat sweet cakes made with bean flour decorated with bits of popped rice colored bright pink and green."

Hi-Jong quickly wiped away her tears. "Not just at New Year's?" she asked, and licked her lips.

"No," Jae-Mi said with a perfectly serious face, "all year long."

Chapter 2

At the harbor in Honolulu the ship anchored and passengers began to climb down a long gangplank to awaiting smaller boats that would take them to a large building on shore. Impatiently, Su-Na and her sisters watched the line of nearly nine hundred Chinese, Japanese, and Korean travelers disembark. When it was finally their turn, Su-Na held tight to her sisters' hands. There were few children on board and she felt as if everyone was watching them. Anxiously, she followed Father, who helped Mother along as she walked with slow steps.

The other passengers, who were mostly men, politely made way for Mother. Like children, women were rare on the ship. In spite of several weeks of illness, Mother looked surprisingly beautiful. With skin like pale clouds and eyes the color of raven's wings, she moved as gracefully as bamboo bent by the wind. Once she self-consciously touched the back of her head. Su-Na knew that Mother was most proud of the beautiful black hair that reached nearly to the back of her knees. She wore it coiled up on her head the way a proper married woman should.

Su-Na watched her Mother walking ahead of her. Like her two sisters, Su-Na had what Mother called "boar's hair," thick and stiff hair that was almost impossible to manage. Su-Na knew that neither she nor her sisters shared their mother's beauty. And this fact, among many others, was clearly a disappointment to Mother. Like almost all Korean women, Mother's marriage had been arranged. She did not meet Father until their wedding day. "It is a pity you are not more attractive," Mother once told Su-Na. "Since we have so little money for your dowry, beauty might certainly help find you a good match."

Su-Na felt perfectly satisfied being exactly the way she was. She had no interest in being married and going off to live in a stranger's house where she would be a slave to a nasty mother-in-law. At this moment she was delighted to be a sojourner in Hawaii, where she did not have to worry about ancient wedding customs. Someday she would return to Korea, but by then her parents might have forgotten about finding her a husband. They could concentrate instead on her sisters.

Su-Na's family and the other Koreans inched into the building, which was filled with long tables and benches. Su-Na laughed when she saw her little sister weaving side to side as she walked.

"There's no spring to solid ground," Jae-Mi declared. She kept expecting to have to lean at the next lurch of the ship. But there was no lurching. She felt oddly unpleasant.

Now that Su-Na was confined in the echoing building, she, too, felt strange. It was strange not to hear the humming of the waves and the thrumming of the engines. The whole world was oddly quiet. The other passengers from the S.S. *Iberia* filed silently into the room and took seats. Were they aware of the changes as well?

"This is where we will eat our first meal," Father said, clearly impressed by the clean, spacious room. "In Hawaii we will be well taken care of." Father was a small, compact man with large, extravagant dreams. He was awake during much of the voyage, excitedly planning their future. He talked constantly about all the things they would accomplish and with what pride his parents would greet them upon their successful return.

Father passed a nearly empty table and motioned for his family to sit at another spot already crowded with Koreans.

"Why not sit here, Father?" Su-Na asked. There were only three other men seated at this table. They did not wear trousers but instead had long robes with wide sleeves.

"Absolutely not. Please do not question my decisions," Father said angrily. He pointed to a bench. "Take a seat."

"Japanese," Mother murmured distastefully.

Father shook his head. "Dwarfish villains."

"What?" Jae-Mi asked and glanced curiously over her shoulder. Except for their clothing, the dwarfish villains looked no different from the hungry Koreans. This was a great disappointment to Jae-Mi. "Are Japanese the same as—"

"Silence!" Father barked. "Stop staring. Turn around."

Jae-Mi did as she was told. Obediently, she and her sisters waited for their dinners. They were surprised to discover that there was no *kimchee*, no Korean rice, no vegetables cooked the way they liked. Instead the meal was simply rice and red fish. Su-Na and her sisters sniffed in fascination. They had never eaten red fish before.

Father signaled that they would begin with a prayer. That accomplished, Su-Na and her sisters began eating with gusto. Only their mother did not seem interested in the food. She picked at the fish with her chopsticks and kept glancing nervously around at their fellow travelers. At home the women never ate with the men. They always ate separately.

Yet here she was sharing a table with complete strangers—close enough to touch sleeves. Would she ever become accustomed to this new life?

"Eat," Father told Mother. "We do not know when we will have a hot meal again."

Mother made a face and put her chopsticks on the table, indicating that she was finished. "Look at this rice! Too dry. The cook must not know anything." She was very proud of the way she cooked rice, a skill she had learned from her mother so that when she moved in with her mother-in-law, she would not be criticized.

"Father, when can we go exploring?" Jae-Mi demanded. She thought the fish was delicious, salty and sweet at the same time. "When do we see our new house?"

"And our new clothes and shoes," Hi-Jong added eagerly.

"Enough!" Father said. "Eat when you eat. Talk when you finish." He scowled at his talkative daughters. They had been in Hawaii only a few hours and already he felt as if he were losing control.

Meekly, the girls finished eating and placed the chopsticks on the table. Mother pouted and stared at her fine hands. They all jumped when a man with a loud voice shouted in a language they did not understand.

"What's he saying, Father?" Su-Na asked.

"He speaks Chinese," Father said. "He's calling names. I think he is taking roll to see if everyone is here and accounted for. Come, we will go closer so that I can hear him call our name."

Father stood up and gathered their belongings. He signaled for his wife and daughters to follow him. The man with the loud voice divided the passengers into groups to be sent to different plantations on different islands. Father and most of his friends from Seoul were sent to the Ewa Plantation on the island of Oahu. Each man lined up to have his name marked in a book and to receive a small metal disc with a number. They were warned to keep these discs safe.

"We will not go to a different island. We will take the train," Father said, beaming. He tucked the disc carefully in his pocket.

"The train?" Mother was shocked. This sounded dangerous. They had never been on a train before. "What if we are killed?"

"Don't worry. It's safe," Father replied. "We'll simply follow the crowd."

Su-Na and her sisters stayed close to Father's heels as he made his way to the long steel path. They waited nervously until an enormous metal snake snorted and smoked directly toward them.

Mother clenched her eyes shut. Su-Na held tight to her sisters. Only Jae-Mi fearlessly studied the monstrous train. "Get on. Hurry," Father said once the train stopped and the doors opened.

Mother seemed frozen, so Su-Na pushed her sisters

forward. They climbed the steps into the train and discovered a long, narrow room with hard, wooden seats. The hot, airless room was crowded with other nervous passengers squeezed elbow to elbow into seats. Father almost had to carry Mother onto the train, she was so terrified. "Sit," he said. Su-Na and her sisters lowered themselves into empty spaces. Mother did the same. As soon as Mother sat, she began to pray.

Without warning, a deafening bell rang. The narrow room lurched and rocked faster and faster. Mother prayed louder and louder. "Look!" Jae-Mi cried. She pointed at the windows where limbless trees flew past so quickly they seemed to lean halfway to the ground. Luxurious, green countryside rushed past. Here snow never fell and cold winds never blew. "Oh," Jae-Mi whispered, "isn't this like the Garden of Eden?"

Father smiled at her, but no one else paid any attention. Mother and Hi-Jong were too frightened to look out the window. Su-Na caught a glimpse of people speeding past. All kinds of people. None of them seemed to be Korean. This surprised Su-Na. Some wore broad hats; others had strangely pale faces. She spied people standing in green fields. They had dark skin and bright clothing. Some of the women wore large pieces of fabric wrapped around their heads. Some didn't. They rode horses and waved at the train, their mouths open and their bright white teeth showing in the way that was forbidden among women at home. One of the women twirled around and around with a man.

Su-Na stared, even though she knew it was rude. *What strange manner of women are these?* She wondered how they had escaped from their homes and were allowed to travel alone in broad daylight. Proper Korean women in veils could only go out after the curfew bell had sounded in town and all the men were off the streets. They were never allowed to be seen dancing with men in public.

"Look at her!" Jae-Mi said.

"Don't wave to those evil creatures," Mother warned. Her eyes were wide open and her expression was one of shock.

The train howled and rocked and shot forward. Mother gripped the worn seat. There were no people on the train car except other Koreans and so the voices and people were familiar. But somehow this did not soothe Mother, who seemed anxious and suspicious of everyone and everything.

Green, lush hills sped past. "Hawaii is even more beautiful than I had imagined," Father said.

The cattle were fat and plentiful in fenced-in places. The air that blew in through the open train window carried the smells of fragrant flowers. The houses they passed were small, only one or two stories high. They seemed to be built of wood and straw and were dull cream colored. Bright green grass carpeted the front of these houses, surrounded by bright flowers and blossoming shrubs. Su-Na wondered if they would live in such a beautiful house.

Much too quickly for Jae-Mi, the train ride ended. Jae-Mi and Hi-Jong clutched their father's hands as they stepped off the train onto the wooden platform. Here another man with a loud voice bellowed for the immigrants to climb onto another train car. This car had no walls, no windows, and no proper seats. It was just a flat shelf with wheels. Father said it was used to haul sugarcane from the fields to the mill. None of the girls knew what this meant. They took a seat in the middle of the car as other passengers scrambled up the sides. Mother followed them awkwardly.

Jae-Mi decided it would be exciting to sit in the open and speed along. She was disappointed to discover that this train crawled slowly along the track.

"What's this?" Su-Na asked. She picked up a green stalk that was mostly stripped of its broad leaves. There were many such stalks scattered on the train car. At one end the stalk oozed something white and sticky. When Su-Na touched it and licked her fingers, the sap tasted sweet.

"Sugarcane," Father said. He smiled and pointed to the great green stalks rising up on all sides of the track. Row upon row of tall cane whispered in the wind. In the distance great smokestacks reached nearly to the sky, higher than any building back home. There was a sweet, burning smell in the air.

The black smoke curling up from the smokestacks

reminded Hi-Jong of the guardian dragon painted on the temple door back home. "Are there dragons here?" she asked hopefully.

"No," Father said, and laughed. "That is the sugar mill."

"Oh," Hi-Jong replied. So far Hawaii had been a great disappointment. No bright clothing, no new shoes, no sweet rice cakes, and no dragons. She had not spied one hat sprouting from the ground or one bolt of silk dangling from a tree. Once again she wondered if the grown-ups had deceived her.

"We're almost there. Our new house looks very fine, doesn't it?" Father said with great enthusiasm. He pointed in the distance to a row of whitewashed cabins that reflected the late-afternoon sun.

The girls nodded. Mother shrugged and sighed. Finally the train car stopped. The man with the loud voice gave directions. The Korean workers filed off to their camp in the east. The Chinese marched to the north and the Japanese hurried to the west. In the center was the mill and another group of buildings.

"There are more Japanese and Chinese than Koreans," Su-Na said to Father.

Father nodded and made a clicking noise with his tongue as if he thought this were a great pity.

Su-Na cleared her throat. "Everywhere we go we travel together, and yet we never speak to them. Why is that, Father?"

Father grunted and picked up their roll of bedding.

"Is it because we do not understand each other's language?" Su-Na asked, remembering the Chinese man in the dining hall who called out names. "If we knew each other's language do you think —"

"Silence!" Father said impatiently. "Must you ask so many questions? It is unseemly for a girl. Now help your mother."

Su-Na frowned as soon as Father turned away from her. She grabbed Jae-Mi and Hi-Jong by the hands and hauled them off the train. In paradise there was supposed to be no confusion, no unhappiness. *Why do I feel so mixed up?*

Jae-Mi wiped grime from her face. Like her sisters, she was dirty and hot. They had been traveling forever. She wondered if they would ever have a home again. Out of nowhere a man galloped up to them on a fine white horse. He waved his brown, American-style hat and smiled at them. He spoke Korean and told them that his name was Boss Jung. "This way, my fellow countrymen," he announced. Father and the other new Korean workers appeared to be relieved. "I have been in Hawaii three years. I am the all-around man here. Interpreter, camp boss, preacher, mail carrier, and language teacher."

The crowd laughed. Boss Jung held up a small metal disc with a number stamped on it. "Do not lose your *bango*," he said. "This is how you will be paid every month. No *bango*, no pay. From now on, this will be your new name. You work hard, *hana-hana*, and you do all right."

Father stared at the *bango* in his hand. Slowly, he repeated aloud: "46571." This was Father's new name.

"*Hana-hana*," Su-Na whispered. She stared out at the cane fields and could see the men and some women moving along the rows. Some were hoeing, others were chopping down the ripe cane. "There are women, Father. Do they have *bangos*, too?"

Father rubbed his chin thoughtfully. "I suppose. And I suppose they are paid, as well."

"Perhaps I should work in the fields. We will need the money," Mother said in a quiet voice.

Father's face darkened. "Even if we have to starve, I will not have you working in the fields."

Mother did not mention her suggestion again. She meekly followed Father to the row of cabins, one of which would be their new home. Unlike the Uncles and Second Uncles, who shared a long barracks-style house, the few married men with families had their own small houses. Su-Na's family's house had a thatched roof made of grass.

They slipped off their shoes the same way they did at home and stepped high over the doorstep to make sure that no unfortunate luck followed them inside. The floor was hard-packed dirt. Inside the one small room there was no furniture, only a shallow fire pit. A scorpion with many legs hurried across the floor.

Mother gasped and scurried out again. Father had to hunt in all the dark corners and up and down every wall to prove to her that there were no more ferocious beasts waiting to ambush her. "See?" he said, smiling. "All gone." He handed a broom made of twigs to Su-Na. Su-Na and her sisters swept the place clean and unrolled the bedding. The family was so exhausted, they did not bother to eat anything for dinner and quickly fell asleep.

It came as a great shock the next morning when the plantation siren blasted at five o'clock. *Br-r-row-aw-ie-ur-ur-rup!*

Shrill voices echoed through the camp. Someone shouted in English and banged on the cabin door. *"Hana-hana, hana-hana,* work, work." Suddenly the door to the cabin swung open. A huge white-skinned *luna* burst in, screaming and cursing. The foreman grabbed the blankets off Father. Mother screamed. Su-Na hid under her blanket with her sisters. *"Hana-hana, hana-hana,"* the *luna* shouted and left.

Father quickly pulled on his work clothes and hurried outside. Su-Na crept to the doorway and watched as up and down the row of cabins the laborers appeared from the shadows like ghosts. They coughed and lit cigarettes. Few spoke. Some carried hoes. She strained her eyes to see her father, but he was soon swallowed up in the gangs of workers. It was clear that no one would be allowed to lie under a palm or a bread tree and do nothing.

Even food was not free. As soon as Su-Na and her sisters finished helping Mother roll up the bedding and carry water from the pump, they had to accompany her to the plantation store. Mother needed a bag of rice and a small crock of *kimchee*. "What number?" the store clerk demanded. He only knew a few words of Korean.

"Number?" Mother asked shyly.

"*Bango* number," Su-Na whispered. "It's 46571," she told the clerk. Carefully, she studied the way he wrote down the number and the cost of their food supplies.

"How do we know he doesn't cheat us?" Mother hissed as they turned to leave with the supplies.

Su-Na pushed open the door. "We don't," she said. "Even though we are only staying here a short while, perhaps we should learn to speak English."

Mother frowned. "Your father would not like that. But then, of course, he must realize that we have to survive as best we can." She gave Su-Na a sly look. "I know you will learn quickly."

"Me?" Su-Na asked. This burden seemed unfair. "What about Jae-Mi and Hi-Jong?"

"They will learn, too. As soon as I can, I am enrolling all three of you in school. Now come along, little pigeons," Mother said. Before Su-Na or her sisters could protest, Mother hurried ahead of them with great determination.

Chapter 3

Luckily for Su-Na and her sisters, there was no school on the plantation. So they had their mother to themselves all day. On the boat she had been too sick to entertain them. At home in Korea she was always busy with tasks given to her by Grandmother, father's mother. But in Hawaii there were few chores. Mother seemed so happy, Su-Na forgot about looking for a new brother under a palm leaf. Mother seemed to enjoy singing them funny old songs with verses like:

Ari-rang. Ari-rang. A-ra-ri-yo.
He is going over Ari-ray Hill
Since he leaves me all alone
He'll have a pain in his foot without
    going very far . . .

Mother told them folk tales about an ambitious mole who lived underground and a proud *miryek*, a statue that raised his head high to the heavens. "All fathers and mothers think their children are perfect," Mother began while they all sat under a tree in the cool shade near their house. "Even the porcupine proclaims its little ones are pleasant and smooth to the touch. But Mole's daughter was truly a dragon child. Her skin was like softest satin, and her little nose and claws were delicately pointed. She was a perfect mole."

"Am I perfect?" Hi-Jong demanded.

"Hush," Jae-Mi said. "What happened next?"

"Little Mole's father decided it was time to find her a husband. But where could he find one perfect enough for his dear daughter? 'She deserves the best in the universe,' Father Mole said. 'Even the Mole King is looked down on by the sky. So I suppose I will travel to the Sky King.'

"When he went to the Sky King, the Sky King said, 'I am not the all-highest. The Sun rules me. The Sun says when I should be bright or dark. Go find the Sun if you want the all-highest.'"

"He will be burned," Hi-Jong muttered. She sat cross-legged with one elbow on each knee.

"But when Mole came to the Sun, the Sun said, 'Cloud is all powerful. He tells me when my face will be bright or dark. Go find Cloud.' Mole found Cloud, but Cloud sent him to Wind. 'Wind drives us clouds across the broad sky.'

"Mole found Wind, who bends the trees. 'There is one thing over which I have no power, even if I puff and blow,' Wind said. 'It is the stone *miryek.*' When Mole went to the statue, the statue said, 'It's true no one can melt me or burn me or blow me over. But there is one creature I fear.'

"'Who?'"demanded Mole.

"'It is a mole.'"

"How can that be?" Hi-Jong demanded. "A mole is only a small creature who lives underground."

Mother put a finger to her lips. "The stone statue told Mole that he and he alone could topple him if he dug long enough and hard enough. So Mole was pleased and went home and told his wife and they arranged a marriage with a fine, handsome young mole to be their daughter's husband. And I am sure that they chose wisely, that the young couple lived happily together, and that they had many sons in their underground home."

"Is this a true story?" demanded Hi-Jong.

"Of course not," Su-Na replied.

Hi-Jong frowned. "Why do the parents always decide?"

"What do you mean?" Mother asked.

"I think she's asking why do the parents always decide who will marry whom," Su-Na said.

Hi-Jong nodded emphatically. "Wind was good. He should have picked Wind."

"A mole can't marry the wind," Jae-Mi announced in a superior voice. "They're not the same."

Mother sighed. "It is a tradition, Su-Na. Our ancestors have arranged marriages for years and years. That's just the way it is."

Su-Na did not feel satisfied with this answer. "What if the parents make a mistake?"

Mother leaned back against the tree and closed her eyes. "Then the couple just learns to get along, that's all."

At the end of the day the great horn blew again. Father trudged home. When he stumbled through the doorway, his hands were bloody and wrapped in rags.

"What happened?" Mother demanded. She sent Su-Na for water.

"Nothing," Father said. Gingerly, he soaked his hands and allowed Mother to bandage them properly.

"I suppose a tailor's hands aren't tough enough for heavy field work," Mother said.

"I will be fine tomorrow," Father said wearily. As if to prove what he said was true, Father rose early and left the house for work even before the siren screamed. Clearly, he did not want to be embarrassed by the *luna*. How humiliating for the overseer to come in and wake his whole family again.

Each night Father spoke in front of the girls about his work. He tried to sound cheerful, even when he had to admit to Hi-Jong that there were no clothes blooming on bushes and no sweet cakes free for the taking here in Hawaii. There were no idle days of doing nothing for Father. Even so, he adamantly refused that either Mother or the girls be allowed to help in the fields.

"I will not permit it," he said, his face stern. There was no arguing with him, even though he could plainly see that the little brown envelope filled with sixteen silver dollars shrank each month. Every time he was paid, money was removed from the envelope for the food supplies they had purchased that month from the plantation store. Father never spoke of his disappointment, but it was clear from the way he walked, shoulders slumped forward, that he was becoming discouraged.

Days passed. The cane grew high. While Father worked cutting and hoeing all day, Su-Na and her sisters helped with chores around the house. Most of the time they played in the yard because they were warned not to wander in the plantation camp. At home in Korea, only boys their age could walk in the street, picnic in the hills in spring, fly kites, or go to buy toys in the city markets. Girls were restricted to the house or the inner courtyard.

As a result, it did not seem like a hardship for them to have to stay near the house. Occasionally they would stray slightly from the house and chase each other among the rows of cane. That was as far as they went. Jae-Mi called loudly to her sisters after she hid herself among the thick, tree-high stalks and then they had to try to come to find her—even though Father had warned them not to play among the acres of cane that stretched forever and forever. "You do not want to be lost, do you?"

"Come out!" Jae-Mi shouted one afternoon when Su-Na was hiding. Jae-Mi and her youngest sister had looked and looked for Su-Na and now their voices sounded fearful. "Come out!" Jae-Mi called again.

The cane whispered back. Leaves rustled in the wind. Jae-Mi searched. She did not see Su-Na crouched, peering out at her. For Su-Na, hiding made her feel invisible. Perhaps, she thought, she had actually vanished. She was gone away and could stare at her sisters and they did not know she was looking. The idea of not being seen was very pleasing.

"Su-Na!" howled Hi-Jong, who began to cry. "Come back!"

Hi-Jong's cries might bring Mother from the house, where she was lying on the pallet. She would be angry with them for being disturbed from her nap. Reluctantly, Su-Na stood up, parted the cane, and crept out of hiding.

Her sisters seemed joyful to see her again, as if she'd gone a very long way from home. "Where were you?" Jae-Mi demanded.

And for once Su-Na enjoyed being reunited, as if

she had gone a very long way and been absent for years. She tried to imagine her sisters' pleasure in seeing her again if she were grown up—it was impossible. But she felt a strange happiness. Someday, she vowed, she would go far away so that when her sisters saw her again, they would rejoice.

After the first cane harvest was over, Father announced that they were going on a short trip on their day off. It was Sunday and the entire family would travel by foot to the settlement that had just built a Korean church. Father, who served as a preacher when Boss Jung was unavailable, was excited to see the building that the Korean workers on the Waialua Plantation had helped construct. Father enthusiastically planned and prepared for their trip.

Unfortunately, at the last moment, Mother was too unwell to make such a long walk. "I will stay here," she said. "I cannot walk that far. You take the girls and go. It will be good for them to be in a church again."

Su-Na and her sisters held their breath. They had looked forward to this trip away from the little house where there were so few other children. They wanted to travel and see more of the island. Reluctantly, Father agreed to take the girls with him to the church. As a special treat, he bought them each something called a banana. None of the girls had ever eaten a banana before. He showed them how to peel back the thick, waxy peel. Then they bit into the soft, sweet fruit.

Su-Na ate her banana slowly, savoring each bite. Hi-Jong nibbled quickly, made a face, dropped hers in the dirt and smashed it with her heel when no one was looking. Jae-Mi gobbled the banana as quickly as she could. She gave her younger sister a hard poke when she saw that she had destroyed her treat so that no one else could enjoy it.

When they reached the church, the girls were surprised to see that it was nothing more than a wooden shack with a thatched roof—not any different from the other buildings in the Korean camp. What was different was that everyone was smiling and dressed in clean clothes. There was no *luna*, no talk of *hana-hana*. A few children gathered shyly behind their mothers. But most of the congregation was made up of Uncles and Second Uncles.

When the service and singing ended, Su-Na and her sisters were glad to escape from the stuffy church and go outside into the sunshine again. "Let's explore," Jae-Mi suggested to her sisters. They could see that the grown-up men were going to stand and talk for a very long time before the picnic began. The women were spreading out long cloths on the ground and setting out baskets filled with rice and cooked fish wrapped in newspaper.

"We should help," Su-Na said, motioning toward

the women who had not yet noticed the girls lingering nearby.

"There's plenty of help," Jae-Mi said. "We'll just be gone a minute. No one will notice."

Hi-Jong licked her lips. She was hungry and yet she wondered what was beyond the grove of trees. All morning in church she had heard a loud thrashing and pounding sound beyond the trees and wondered what it was. "Are there dragons?" she asked Su-Na.

"No, of course not," Su-Na said impatiently.

Hi-Jong felt disappointed. She took Jae-Mi's hand and followed her quickly into the shadows. Su-Na trailed behind them.

"We must only be gone a short time," Su-Na called.

The girls worked their way through the dark trees to the thundering noise that grew louder and louder. When the girls came out of the shadows the light was nearly blinding.

"Snow!" Hi-Jong exclaimed, eager to feel the cold white that she remembered from winters in the village.

The three girls rushed onto the beach and soon discovered that the ground was covered with white sand, not snow. They laughed and kicked off their shoes. The sand felt soft beneath their bare feet. Magnificent blue-green waves curled white and dashed against the shore. The beach shuddered with the crash of each wave.

"Dragons," Hi-Jong murmured happily. Wind whipped her hair in her face. When she stuck out her tongue, she could taste something salty flying through the air.

Su-Na paused and held both of her sisters by their hands so that they could not move any closer to the water. "We must go back now."

"No!" Jae-Mi protested. "When will we have a chance like this again? Come on. We'll just touch the waves. They aren't dangerous. We sailed across them, remember?"

The surprising sound of children's voices suddenly filled the air. "Who are they?" Su-Na pointed. Farther down the beach a group of brown-skinned boys and girls about their age ran and tumbled toward the water. They quickly dropped any unnecessary clothes and plunged half-naked into the surf. Snatches of their laughter and shouts could be heard every now and again between the crashing of the waves.

Su-Na and her sister crept closer. At home boys and girls were separated after age seven. Weren't these girls embarrassed? Where were the grown-ups? The strange children flew into the waves, their dark hair streaming down their backs. They splashed and swam, vanished and bobbed up again and again. Since neither Jae-Mi nor her sisters knew how to swim, the sight of such fearless splashing shocked them. Little by little, the current seemed to be pushing the strangers down the beach to the place where Su-Na and her sisters stood gawking.

"It can't be that scary. Look at them. They look like fish," Jae-Mi said admiringly.

A few of the girls laughed and splashed their way to shore. When they noticed Su-Na and her sisters watching, they signaled their companions in a language that Su-Na and her sisters did not understand. Su-Na froze as the strangers came closer. They were dripping with salt water. Their wet hair was plastered against their faces. They were nearly without clothing—something no girl at home would ever try. Their black eyes flashed. Their teeth were very white.

They stared at Su-Na and her sisters and poked them. They sniffed them and prodded them. Su-Na, too scared to move, shut her eyes tight.

"Who are they?" Hi-Jong demanded in a quaking voice. "What do they want?"

"Who are you?" Jae-Mi demanded bravely in Korean.

The strangers only laughed and said something that sounded like rippling water. They lifted Jae-Mi's braids and inspected her dress. Jae-Mi froze, unaccustomed to people looking so closely and intently at her. In Korea it was considered rude for a stranger to inspect another person in this fashion.

"Let go!" Jae-Mi shouted and gave one of the strange girls a push. But instead of becoming angry, the girl simply laughed. She pulled her friends away, back toward the place on the beach where they had dumped their clothes. In a few minutes they returned with a furry-looking brown ball that had been cracked in half. One of the boys pried it open, handed half to his friend, then tilted his half back and gulped noisily.

He wiped his hand on his plump stomach and then scooped out white flesh from the inside of the ball with his fingers. His friends quickly joined him.

"Look at that. They're eating with their fingers," Hi-Jong said with disgust.

One of the strangers dug a piece away and handed it to Jae-Mi.

"Don't eat that," Hi-Jong warned.

"Why not?" Jae-Mi answered. She nibbled a bit. "It's good even if you don't eat it with chopsticks."

Su-Na tasted some. It was better than a banana, she decided. The strange girls watched her and laughed.

Jae-Mi smiled. She wished these ocean girls who seemed more like sleek, strange fish than human beings could understand her. Did they live in the ocean or on the land? Jae-Mi wished she could ask them how they mastered swimming in the water and walking and running on land.

Suddenly from the grove of trees Su-Na heard a loud shout. "Father!" She grabbed her sisters and hurried down the beach. Hi-Jong and Jae-Mi moved their legs as fast as they could back into the trees.

Father stood scowling with his hands on his hips. "You cannot wander off. Ever. I have been looking everywhere," he said angrily. "Who are they?" He pointed to the ocean children, who had drifted away.

"We don't know their names," Jae-Mi said. She dropped the last piece of sweet white fruit behind her back.

Father snorted. "*Kanakas*. Native people. Stay away from them."

"But why?" Hi-Jong asked.

Father turned and glared at her. "They are not Korean. They are not like us. Stay with your own kind." Abruptly he motioned for them to follow him. The girls did as they were told and did not look back.

When the girls trudged home later that afternoon with their Father, they were surprised to discover tacked outside their cabin door a twisted rope with a small piece of charcoal attached. "What is this?" Hi-Jong asked. She knew the rope had not been there when they left. A pair of strange shoes was lined up outside the front door.

"Where is Mother?" Jae-Mi demanded in a panicked voice.

Father did not answer. He smiled broadly as he pushed open the door. Immediately, they were surrounded by the sound of a booming, unfamiliar woman's voice. Su-Na and her sisters crept inside, wondering what had happened while they were gone.

It was unlike Mother to have a visitor. They had no extra money to buy delicacies like a cup of tea to share with a guest. Korean women who worked on the plantation had no time for idle gossip.

"Congratulations!" bellowed Mrs. Lee, a large woman from Ewha. She bowed deeply to Father. She had a broad, friendly face. She motioned to Mother, who was lying on the pallet on the floor. She looked tired but happy. Snuggled beside her was a bright red-faced creature no bigger than a scrawny cat.

"A baby!" Su-Na said. She crept closer for a better look. It squirmed. She knew it was alive. That was a relief.

"A *boy* baby," Mrs. Lee said proudly. "You should be very pleased to have an honored brother."

Hi-Jong and Jae-Mi watched as Mrs. Lee picked up the small, squalling bundle and handed it to Father. All the grown-ups looked delighted.

"Strong lungs. Good," Father said, beaming.

Hi-Jong put her hands over her ears. "Too loud," she said. Jae-Mi nodded in agreement. Their cabin had somehow become even smaller. Every inch seemed filled with the ear-piercing cry of this new stranger.

"You must make some seaweed soup for my son's mother," Father said. He cradled the baby awkwardly in his arms. "She is not to leave the bed for two weeks. You must do everything to help her. Do you understand, Su-Na?"

Su-Na sighed. No more games of tag in the tall cane. No more exploring the beach. This new honored baby was certainly going to be a great deal of trouble, she could tell already.

"Pay your respects to your new brother," Father commanded.

The girls came closer and bowed. The little boy had a withered pink face like an old man. He tilted back his head, his tiny mouth quivered, and he howled.

Hi-Jong did not look impressed. "What is his name?"

"We must first consult the zodiac," Father said. "The proper name can be good luck and assure a long and prosperous life."

Jae-Mi reached out to touch the little pink fist.

"Do not touch him. Your hands are dirty," Mother commanded. "We must take all precautions."

Jae-Mi tucked her hand inside her pocket. Her lip quivered. She wasn't trying to hurt the baby. She was only trying to touch his skin, to see what he felt like.

"Your son seems very hearty to me," Mrs. Lee said to Father. "He is a loud and lusty crier. Now you will not die without an heir."

"The first child to be born in America," Father boasted. "He is certainly a sign of good luck."

Father, Mother, and Mrs. Lee were so busy praising the baby, they did not seem to notice when Su-Na and her sisters shuffled out the door. "He is quite hideous," Jae-Mi said in a low voice.

"Nothing like I expected," Hi-Jong agreed.

"Be glad he was born and hope that he lives long enough to celebrate his *tol* after his first one hundred days," Su-Na said. "There will be lots of food and treats. Maybe presents." She recalled the parties celebrating the birth of her younger cousins.

"When I was born was there much rejoicing?" Hi-Jong asked quietly as she and her sisters began gathering wood for the fire pit.

Su-Na shook her head, then shrugged. "You were a girl."

Chapter 4

Meung, as the new baby was called, grew rapidly. He delighted his parents. He eventually even delighted his sisters, who carried him about to show him the pale orchids and fragrant hibiscus. Wherever they went, they were reminded by Mother, who was now called Mother of Meung, to take a large palm leaf to wave away the flies from the precious face of their only beloved brother.

One afternoon while Hi-Jong and Jae-Mi rocked their little brother in a hammock Father had specially hung between two trees, Su-Na stayed inside with Mother. A package had come from Korea. The brown wrapping was thick and torn. Mother snipped the twine away and carefully peeled back the wrapping. Excitedly, she pulled away the last bit of wrapping. Covered in tissue was a photograph.

"Do you remember, Su-Na?" Mother asked excitedly.

Just before the family left Korea they had had their picture taken. Seeing her grandparents' faces again made Su-Na take a sudden deep breath. At first she could not speak. There they were—all of them—Mother, Father, Grandfather, Grandmother, her two sisters, her aunt, her uncle, and her uncle's wife. All the grown-ups wore white, the color of wisdom. The women, who stood on the left, had their best *han-bok* dresses. Their hair was parted in the middle and gathered in back in the style of married women. Grandmother and Grandfather sat with Su-Na and Hi-Jong on their laps. Jae-Mi, too restless to sit on anyone's lap, stood beside Mother.

"Oh, I remember that day so clearly," Mother said.

Su-Na recalled the waiting and the reprimands. The threats. She had never had her picture taken before but clearly it was an important moment. Why else was everyone so dressed up? Grandfather with his pointed beard and mustache looked so proud, so severe. "Sit still," he kept hissing. Su-Na obeyed. She kept her hands in her lap and did not move even though her linen dress collar bit into her neck and sweat trickled down her arms.

Could the man with the black box see that she had forgotten to wash her ears? He kept waving his hand in the air so that they knew where to look. No one smiled. No one dared. There was a bright flash and then the ordeal was over.

Now when Su-Na studied the picture she noticed how different everyone looked. Mother never wore white anymore. Her dresses were cheap printed shifts made of material she bought at the plantation store. She looked so young and carefree in the photograph. Su-Na peeked at Mother and saw that her face was lined around the mouth and eyes now. But it was Father who was the most changed. He stood so straight and tall in the picture, the proud eldest son. His hair was jet black and neatly parted. She hardly recognized him.

"It is a wonderful picture," Mother whispered. She wiped a tear from her eye. "I am so glad to have it."

Su-Na did not reply. There was such a terrible sadness in Mother's voice. She did not sound at all happy. Mother carefully placed the picture on the low table Father had built for them. Then she went to the wall and pulled a broken board away. From behind the board, she took a tin can. This, Su-Na knew, was where they stored their money. Every month when Father came home with his little brown envelope, she watched her parents carefully place the new coins into the can.

Mother tipped the can and the coins tumbled out on the table with a loud jangling. There were barely half a dozen. She fingered each coin.

"This is all our money?" Su-Na asked, impressed. She had never seen so much money in one place at one time. Certainly they must be very rich.

Mother nodded but she did not smile. She counted the silver dollars quickly, replaced them, and put the can back into its hiding place in the wall. "Every month your father hopes to save enough to send money home for Grandmother's *hwangap*," she said in a hushed voice.

Su-Na knew that Grandmother's sixtieth birthday was a very important, auspicious occasion. When a person turned sixty, she had lived a very long time. It was the custom to celebrate with a very big party with many guests and gifts and all kinds of good food to eat and drink. "Grandmother will be very pleased," Su-Na said.

Mother sighed. "After nearly ten months, we have not been able to send even one dollar," she said. "Life is very expensive here. There are doctors to pay, food to buy, clothing to purchase. We save and save and then something takes the *hwangap* money away. Someday, though, someday we will send money for Grandmother's birthday," Mother said. She stared at the photograph one last time and then she picked up a battered pan half filled with water. She began rinsing the rice before it would be cooked. She swished the rice back and forth, back and forth so that it made a comforting sound. "Soon your father will be coming for dinner. Take him some water to drink when he gets off the train. I'm sure he will be hot and dusty as usual."

Su-Na picked up the drinking gourd and filled it with water from the bucket using the dipper. "Mother?"

Outside came the crying sound of Meung. "Hungry again," Mother murmured. She glanced up impatiently at Su-Na. "Why are you still standing there? Hurry. There is much to get done before dinner."

Su-Na hurried out the door. She did not have the chance to ask Mother when they would return to Korea. *Maybe another time.*

"Where you going?" Jae-Mi called as Su-Na rushed past. Jae-Mi held Meung and jiggled him to hush his crying.

"Train," Su-Na replied and grinned with disdain. For once she was the one who got to escape from baby-sitting chores.

Wind bent the palm trees. Su-Na held the gourd close against herself and leapt carefully along the sandy path, past the other Korean cottages, past the pump where the women were filling buckets with water for the big bathtub. She skirted the Japanese and the Chinese camps the way she had been instructed by Father. "Do not speak to them," he had told her.

"Why?" she asked. She had seen some Chinese children, not many, just about ten or so, playing with sticks and a ball near one of the houses. She wanted to go to see who they were and if perhaps there might be a girl her age. It was tiresome always playing with her younger sisters. But when she asked Father's permission, he became very angry. "If you try to make friends with a tiger, you will end up in his stomach" was his reply.

This did not make sense to Su-Na. She recalled Grandmother's stories about long ago days in Korea, when vicious, striped beasts prowled the high wild peaks and came down to the villages in spring to eat poor, unsuspecting peasants. "Does Mountain Uncle live in Hawaii?" Su-Na had asked, using the honorific name given all stealthy, killer tigers.

"Do not ask so many questions," Father replied with irritation.

Su-Na knew better than to open her mouth again. She would only make Father furious. She stayed away from the Chinese tiger-children and did not bring up the subject again.

Now, she waited patiently beside the tracks where the flat cars rolled in from the fields. She knew Father would be glad to have a sip of water as soon as he stepped off the dusty train. She waited a long time until the track rumbled.

"Hey, *biki, biki!*" a *luna* shouted at her and waved his hat. His face was dirty. His voice had a warning tone. What was he trying to tell her? He shouted again and pointed toward the sky, which was turning a deep bruised color. Like so many of the foremen, his words were a jumble of Korean, Hawaiian, Chinese, and Japanese even though he himself was Portuguese. "Never trust a *haole*," the Uncles always advised each other over the pump. "White people are treacherous."

Su-Na did not know what the *luna* was saying. Anxiously she looked around. A flat car rumbled closer. Even from this distance she could see that it was crowded with men. She scanned the crowd, trying to catch a glimpse of her father. She waited and waited, practicing in her mind all the happy things she would tell him. The picture, she would tell him about the picture. Eagerly she watched and waited.

Finally the last dusty Korean worker climbed off the flat car. He looked like an old man, bent and dusty. His face was darkened by the sun. He scowled and walked with a shuffle, his hands in his pockets, his lunch pail under one arm.

Where is Father?

Another crowded train car rolled into view and stopped. More Koreans climbed off. A few wore traditional white baggy trousers and top jackets tied in front. These white garments had become gray and stained from the field work. An even smaller number of men continued to wear their hair tied up on the top of their heads in a topknot. These same men continued to wear tall horsehair hats that signified that they were special *yangban*, members of the learned upper class back in Korea. As the men hurriedly shuffled off the train, a gust of wind knocked a tall hat from one of the men's heads. The hat rolled away across the dirt and onto the track.

"Ai-goo!" the hat's owner cried. He scurried after the precious hat as it flew out of reach. A few of his fellow workers dodged after the hat to try to help him. But as they did, there was such a commotion that the next flat car could not make it down the tracks.

"Get out of the way!" the *luna* screamed in English. He galloped up on his horse and flung his whip in all directions. "What's going on here?"

The wind blew harder and the hat tumbled off the tracks and into the cane field. The men chased after the hat. The cursing *luna* rode after the men. After a few moments the chagrined workers returned to the flat car and removed their belongings from the track. The hat was gone.

The red-faced *luna* shouted more instructions. It was Boss Jung who finally calmed the crowd and made the announcement. "My friends," Boss Jung said. "No more hats to work. No more topknots. This is not Korea. If you do not obey, you will lose your jobs. Understand?"

The *luna* grumbled again at Boss Jung. He wanted to make sure that all his instructions had been given.

Boss Jung nodded and sighed. It was an unpopular order, but what could he do? He was only following directions.

The Korean workers grumbled. They trudged away as the rain began to fall in large fat drops. The next flat car rolled to a stop. More men climbed off. Su-Na scanned the crowd again. "Father?" she called.

The last man to climb off the flat car glanced up. His expression was startled, as if he had just woken from a dream. It took a few moments for him to recognize Su-Na. He managed to smile and wave. "Little dragon, how are you?" he greeted her. The wind began to blow. The cane shook.

She handed him the water gourd. Immediately he took a few long swallows. Then he wiped his face with the back of his hand and thanked her. He took her hand in his hard, calloused fingers. Together they walked back to their house. Father seemed too tired to speak. Su-Na walked silently. All she could think about was the *luna* with the whip. But she could not speak of that unpleasantness. In all the commotion she completely forgot about the photograph from Korea.

This was the first time since they had come to Hawaii that she had had her father to herself. *Say something.* Back home, they would often spend time together having poetry contests. Father would speak a *sijo* poem and she would answer with another. This used to please him. Before Father had a son, it seemed to give him pleasure to hear Su-Na recite ancient poetry—something he loved, too. "You are very like your father," Mother used to say. "Perhaps that is why you make him so angry sometimes."

Nervously, she cleared her throat and recited the first poem she remembered:

"At the first sign of my horse's fright,
I tightened the reins and looked down.
Green mountains in silken splendor
Stood submerged in water.
Poor horse, do not be frightened,
I only came to look."

Father paused and glanced at her. "Very good, *Poksili,*" he said, using her pet name from when she was a very little girl.

"Now you, Father. You say one," Su-Na said. She felt pleased to be called "Happy." No one had called her that in a very long time.

"Let me see," Father said, and tapped his forehead.

"Butterflies playing happily
In a hundred-flowered garden,
Beware. Though each fragrance lures you,
Try not to land on every flower.
Sunset may find you
Entangled in a spider web."

From somewhere in the house came the sound of Meung howling. "Your brother's calling," Father said happily. Before she could tell Father that she, too, wrote poetry and suggest that someday perhaps he might like to read it, he was already hurrying toward the house.

Too late. Su-Na sighed and followed him.

Later that night, when their parents thought they were asleep, Su-Na listened as her parents whispered. "Like machines," Father murmured. "There were two hundred of us workers and seven or eight *lunas* and above them a field boss on a horse. We are watched constantly. *Biki, biki!* Hurry, hurry! They shout all day. Hoe, hoe, hoe for four hours in a straight line and no talking. Hoe every weed along the way to your three rows. Hoe—chop chop chop, one chop for one small weed, two for all the big ones."

Mother rubbed his back. He had to remain bent over, he said, all day. He whispered how they ached to stand up and stretch and unknot their twisted bodies, to feel the freedom of arched backs. "We curse the *lunas*, hollering and swearing at us for not working fast enough," Father said. "At home we had names. Our names told us who we were, connected us to family and community. Here we are treated no better than horses or cows."

Su-Na tried to keep her eyes open. Phrases floated through the room.

"A better day . . ."
"And what of that?"
"Enough rice."
"No future here."
"The money we owe."
"There is only so much . . ."

Su-Na did not dare whisper a word to her sisters. What were their parents saying? She felt sorry for her father that he had to work so hard. This was the first time she had ever heard him complain. Perhaps, she told herself, he had only had a bad day. A very bad day. Tomorrow would be better. That was what he always said. They only had to keep hoping for the best.

Yet, try as she might, she could not keep her heavy eyelids open. She was soon sound asleep.

Chapter

5

Riverside, California

1906

My way cannot be far since
I hear the sound of thunder.
Look high on the mountaintop
Under white clouds, they told me.
But how will I ever find refuge
With all these clouds floating around me?

Father said the place they were going was called Riverside. *Riverside.* Jae-Mi said this word over and over to herself and wondered what it meant. "Where is Riverside?"

"California," Su-Na explained to her one afternoon

as the three sisters carried water in buckets from the plantation pump to their house.

"Where is California?" Hi-Jong demanded. Her lip quivered. Once again she had been tricked by grown-ups. Once again they were changing everything just when she had finally become accustomed to this place.

"California is America," Su-Na explained. She shot a glance at her youngest sister and hoped she wasn't going to cry again.

Jae-Mi jammed the bucket under the pump spout and began to push the pump handle with all her might. "I don't want to go. I like Hawaii. America is too big."

"America," Su-Na explained slowly, copying the words she had heard her parents use, "is better. We will have many more opportunities. We will be able to go to school and improve ourselves."

"I don't want to go to school," Jae-Mi replied. She crouched on the ground beside the bucket and cupped her hands around a spider. "I like to be outside barefoot all day in warm sunshine. Can I do that in Riverside? Is there ocean? Are there bananas?"

Su-Na shrugged. She wasn't sure. "America is better. Father said."

"How do we get there?" Jae-Mi demanded.

"Ship," Su-Na said. "We have to cross more ocean."

"Not again!" Hi-Jong declared. Her expression

crumpled. She could remember the feeling of being seasick. Why did she have to endure that again? It was too terrible. She would rather stay here instead. Grunting loudly, she sat on the ground and rubbed her dirty hands against her dress. "You don't tell the truth, Su-Na. Why should we believe you?"

Su-Na looked at her pouting sister with surprise. "What do you mean?"

Hi-Jong shot Jae-Mi a conspiratorial glance. "Tell her."

"Remember? You said we would have sweet New Year cakes made of bean flour every day," Jae-Mi said, her eyes narrowing. "We have not had such treats even once since we've been here. And there are no shoes, no fancy clothes blossoming on branches."

Su-Na coughed nervously. "That was the Uncles. They told you that."

"Do you mean to say the Uncles are liars just like you?" Jae-Mi demanded.

Su-Na scratched the back of her neck and tried not to look into her sisters' eyes. She carefully rebraided the end of one braid and tied it with a piece of old twine. "We have already bought our tickets. Father has paid back what he owes for our steamship passage here to the plantation. He has found a good job in Riverside. It is settled. Do not be disrespectful."

Still, Hi-Jong and Jae-Mi refused to budge. They

sat beside the sandy path and eyed their eldest sister suspiciously.

"Do not be ungrateful," Su-Na said impatiently. "America is the land of opportunity. Come, Mother is waiting."

When she finally managed to coax her sisters home, they discovered that Father had cut his hair nearly as short as the priests back home. He bought a new pair of American blue pants and a white shirt for the journey. He purchased an American-style dress for Mother, who seemed pleased but bewildered.

"Father!" Su-Na declared in surprise. Her sisters peered cautiously at Father as if he might have become a stranger.

"We are going to America. We must look like Americans," Father said. He smiled broadly. He looked happier than he had in a very long time. Su-Na and her sisters did not know why, but they felt happy, too.

"Prospects for the future are better in America," Mother said. "Wages are ten to fifteen cents an hour for ten hours' work a day."

Su-Na remembered the coffee can behind the wall filled with so few coins. She thought of what Mother had told her about Grandmother's birthday and what she had overheard about Father's aching back. Maybe Riverside would be their only chance.

During the next two days, the family said their good-byes to Mrs. Lee and their other neighbors. Su-

Na and her sisters packed up their small treasures. Jae-Mi found a small pink shell. Su-Na pressed a wildflower among her poems about ocean, wind, and sky. Hi-Jong asked her mother if she could take a starfish. When the spiny creature began to stink, Father made her throw it back among the trees.

Su-Na asked Father what he planned to take from Hawaii to America and he said, "Nothing. Not even this." In his fist he showed her the *bango* with his number. He seemed delighted by the idea of heaving this, too, into the trees, as if by doing so he had rid himself of an unpleasant former identity.

"Are we ready?" Mother said with great exuberance on the day of their departure. Father helped her tuck blankets around Meung for their journey by train back to Honolulu. Su-Na's parents' enthusiasm was contagious enough to convince her sisters. Their camp neighbors came to say a last good-bye. "Lucky ones!" they said. "We will come to America, too."

When they arrived in Honolulu, they found their ship, called the S.S. *China,* waiting at the dock. It was an enormous American ship with an American crew and Chinese cooks. Su-Na's family hurried below to steerage class, which was crowded with Koreans and Japanese. "Good-bye, aloha land!" Jae-Mi called to the many people waving handkerchiefs on the dock. The ship's loud whistle pierced the air and they were on their way.

It took seven days to reach the mainland, as America was called. Every day Su-Na and her sisters checked for signs of the great new place they would call home. Every day Father stood on deck holding Meung proudly in his arms. He said he wanted his eldest son to be there to witness this important moment. Only Mother, who was seasick, stayed below.

Finally one foggy morning in May the ship's whistle blew. In the distance Su-Na heard the loud bellowing sound of an enormous frog. "What is that, Father?" she asked worriedly.

"A warning to the ship of treacherous waters," he said. He kept careful watch on his daughters that afternoon. The rumor among the steerage passengers was that they were soon to enter San Francisco Bay. The ship moved slowly as tugboats appeared on either side to guide it into shallower waters. Su-Na and her sisters peered out and tried to see San Francisco but the city was covered with fog. Every so often they caught glimpses of what looked like hills.

"Where is the city?" Jae-Mi demanded.

"We must not be impatient," Father said. He scanned the bay anxiously. "The pilot knows what he's doing."

After a while the medical inspector from the Immigration Service came on board. He lined up all the steerage passengers on deck in three separate groups. Su-Na's family joined the Koreans, who all looked terrified. The inspector marched up and down the line. "He holds the key to America," one of the nearby Koreans whispered. "He may let you land or send you home."

"Here he comes," his companion replied. "Well, if it's a beating you are to get, sooner the better to get it over with."

Meung began to cry. Mother rocked him in her arms. Meanwhile, Father fumbled with his coat sleeves. Su-Na could see that he was trying his best to cover up the pus marks from the lingering infection on his hands and wrists—the result of sharp cane injuries. Fortunately the health inspector did not notice. The translator asked Father where they were going to settle. Did they have any money? Did they have proof of a job? Did they realize there were no jobs in San Francisco and nowhere for them to stay? Did they know they must keep their immigration papers with them at all times in America or risk being sent back?

Father bowed respectfully and answered each question. He seemed relieved when the health inspector quickly glanced over Mother, the baby, and Su-Na and her sisters. "That was not so bad," Father said. "You see Americans are very polite."

Mother did not say anything. The fog had lifted and now they could see for the first time something of San Francisco from where they were standing on deck. The city looked ghostly and strange. "Father," Jae-Mi asked, "what is wrong with the buildings?"

Su-Na and Hi-Jong peered into the distance and they, too, sensed that something terrible had happened here. The white brick walls stood askew as if they had been partially knocked down. The crumbling brick walls looked like bad teeth and everywhere was the smell of smoke.

"Earthquake," Father said in a quiet voice. "In April—just a month ago. Nearly three thousand people died. Thousands more lost their homes."

"What is an earthquake?" Su-Na demanded.

"A terrific rumbling and shifting of the earth. They have them in Japan. Buildings fell down, many burned. I have heard that they are already rebuilding the city," Father said in as reassuring a voice as he could muster. "Do not worry. We are not staying here. Where we are going is far from San Francisco."

Su-Na felt a shiver run down her spine. Why had they come to this place? America was falling apart. How did Father know that it wasn't the same in Riverside?

"What happens if the earthquake returns when we step on shore?" Jae-Mi demanded. Nervously, she scanned the hillsides. Couldn't the great cracks swallow people as well as buildings?

"Do not worry," Father said. "We are only going to be here a short while. Long enough to reach the train and then we shall be on our way."

Mother smiled bravely. Somehow Su-Na and her sisters sensed that she, too, was terrified.

A shout rang out on deck and the group of Korean and Japanese passengers filed down the gangplank. When it was the family's turn to walk down the platform to the dock, Su-Na saw many people milling about. At first they looked very small, very strange. Their faces were pale and they had angry expressions. Some of the men were shaking their fists at the passengers and calling words Su-Na did not understand.

"Is this the polite way Americans greet strangers?" Mother whispered to Father.

Father took the baby in his arms, his jaw muscles tightening. "Su-Na, take your sisters' hands. Do not stop. Do not even pause for one moment. Follow me closely."

Now Su-Na felt terrified, too. There was no turning back. The crowd spilling down off the ship pushed forward. Su-Na and her family had no choice but to keep walking toward the shouting people on the dock. What were they saying?

"Keep moving," Father warned.

Su-Na held her sisters' hands as tightly as she could. She followed Father and Mother. Now she could see the Americans' faces up close and she was truly terrified. Some laughed derisively. Some pointed and hooted. They seemed more like wild dogs than people. "Jap! Jap!" they barked. *What do they mean?*

Su-Na tried not to look at them. She wished she could vanish into thin air. *What is this word?*

Suddenly someone spit.

"Father!" Jae-Mi called. She watched, horrified, as a white glob trailed down the back of Father's new American shirt.

Father did not stop. "Quiet. Do not look at them," Father called to the girls as he kept walking ahead of them. "Keep moving."

They were nearly off the loading platform. They were just about to step onto the dock and onto solid ground when a man darted out from the crowd past the rope barrier. Su-Na watched as if he were moving in slow motion. He came closer and closer so that she could see his greasy hat, his whiskered pale face, his bloodshot, angry eyes. And then he did something so incredible, Su-Na could hardly believe what she was seeing. The man reached down and tore Mother's cotton skirt. This stranger simply wrenched it in his hands and ripped it as easily as if it had been paper. Then he shouted something horrible and dove off into the crowd again and vanished.

Mother stumbled. Father took her firmly by the elbow and kept moving. Not knowing what else to do, Su-Na followed. She felt people behind her, stepping on her heels, whispering to keep moving, as if it were all her fault. The whole time Jae-Mi and Hi-Jong wanted to catch up with their mother, they wanted to see if she was all right. But they couldn't because of the crowd, because of the way Father kept moving. Meung looked back at them over Father's shoulders and his eyes were wide and wise and there was something so awful to Su-Na about seeing that helpless baby and Father's back spattered with spit.

Su-Na walked faster. She could hear Father's voice. She could see him look at Mother. And Su-Na knew Father was afraid. *It isn't true that nothing bad can ever happen to us in America.* At that moment something took hold of Su-Na, some energy, and she felt herself pushing her sisters along very quickly. She did not hear them telling her to slow down. She did not hear Hi-Jong shriek that she had lost her shell. She just kept pushing them forward, ever forward, away from the danger, away from the men in the crowd who pressed in on them from all sides for no reason.

When they finally reached the safety of the crumbling, half-destroyed train station, Su-Na sat down on a packing crate. Her legs shook uncontrollably. She could not look at Mother, whose hair was undone and sticking out in all directions. "I am all right," Mother reassured them. Her face was pale. Her lips were pale. Her eyes seemed enormous and baffled. She stared at her daughters as if she hardly recognized them.

"We are all still together. We are all still alive," Father said. His voice quavered. He, too, looked shaken.

Su-Na felt as if she might throw up. She put an arm

around Hi-Jong, who buried her face in Su-Na's lap. Only Jae-Mi refused to sit down. Instead she paced back and forth. "Why do they hate us?" she demanded angrily. "What have we done to deserve this?"

Father took a deep breath. "When the first white missionaries came to Korea, they were treated equally badly. They were cursed by our people even though they came in peace to do good works. But the Korean people, when they saw them for the first time, thought they were different. They looked strange. They called them 'white devils.' Even children threw rocks." Father paused. "Anything new and strange causes some fear at first. Ridicule and violence often result."

Hi-Jong began to whimper. "Why have we come to a place where we are not wanted? What is 'Jap'? Why did they keep shouting that word?"

Father glanced quickly at Mother. "It is a terrible word. A word meant to hurt someone. Someone who is Japanese."

Jae-Mi clenched her fists and felt even more confused. "They think we are Japanese?"

"Ignorance," Father said slowly. "You must understand the Americans are frightened. They have just suffered a terrible earthquake. Their homes, their jobs are gone. It must seem like the end of the world."

"They deserve it," Jae-Mi said angrily. "I would like to hurt them for what they did to you and Mother."

Father bit his lip. "You cannot."

"Why? They tried to hurt us."

"More violence will not solve anything," Father said quietly. "What happened to us is exactly the same thing that happened to the missionaries."

Jae-Mi stared at her father in puzzlement. What did missionaries have to do with spit on his back and Mother's ripped skirt? He made no sense.

"The missionaries did not react to their tormentors," Father continued. "They simply lowered their heads and paid no attention. We must do the same thing."

Jae-Mi paced more rapidly. "I don't understand. What must we do?"

Mother, who had been quiet until this moment, suddenly spoke. "We must work hard and study hard and learn to show Americans that we are just as good as they are."

No one said a word. Jae-Mi shook her head. She still did not feel convinced. What had they ever done to deserve such violent, unfair treatment? They weren't Japanese. Couldn't these Americans tell the difference?

Su-Na's shoulders slumped forward. She stroked Hi-Jong's hair. It was one thing to be a grown-up and say such brave words. But what could a small girl like Su-Na or her sisters do? Mother's advice seemed impossible. Yet there she sat, telling them what to do. And she was the one with the torn skirt. The one who had not only been spit upon but touched, violated.

What was even more bewildering was Father. She had heard him use a hurtful phrase to describe the Japanese. *Dwarfish villain.* Had he already forgotten?

Father helped Mother clean off her skirt. He held the baby and rocked him while she went into the train station's public lavatory. "The train will be here soon. We will have a nice, long ride. You'll see," Father said in his most cheerful voice. "Everything will be better in Riverside. There are citrus groves there filled with sweet oranges and lemons. A pleasant little house. Plenty of work. Plenty to eat. Now don't worry."

Su-Na wanted to believe him. *Doesn't he know every-thing?* Somehow she wasn't sure anymore. All that she was certain of was her desire to leave America and go back to Korea. But how could they do that? She knew they had used every bit of money they had for their passage here.

Every so often Jae-Mi glanced toward the lavatory door where Mother had disappeared. What if something happened to her in there? What if there were more of those angry people waiting to hurt her simply because she was different?

"I want to go back," Hi-Jong mumbled into the folds of Su-Na's rumpled skirt.

"Back to Korea?" Su-Na said in a soothing voice.

Hi-Jong avoided looking at her sister. "I want to go back to Hawaii."

Chapter

6

Wind last night blew down
A gardenful of peach blossoms.
A boy with a broom
Is starting to sweep them up.
Fallen flowers are flowers still;
Don't brush them away.

Jae-Mi felt lost in such a huge country. The train seemed to travel forever. When she looked out the window, the scenery looked exactly as it had hours before. Gray-green scrub, yellow soil, low hills. Perhaps they weren't even moving. Perhaps they hadn't gone anywhere at all. *Kae-guk chinch-wi.* She reminded herself. "The country is open, go forward." Even saying these words did not seem to help.

When Jae-Mi looked around the train car she saw

many of the same people she had seen on the ship from Hawaii. Koreans, Chinese, and Japanese were all traveling together. She felt restless and wanted to ask a question that had been bothering her for the past hour. But she did not wish to wake Mother, who was holding sleeping Meung. Father sat with Hi-Jong in the seat ahead of them. His head was leaning against one hand with his elbow propped against the window. He appeared to be lost in thought.

Jae-Mi tugged Su-Na's sleeve. Her sister was dozing off in the hard, worn upholstered seat beside her. "Where are the others?" Jae-Mi whispered.

"Others?"

"The Americans. Where are they?"

Su-Na yawned. "They are in the car ahead of us."

"What kind of car is that? I saw you peek in there before Father stopped you."

"A nice, comfortable, first-class car with soft seats."

"Why do we not travel in the first-class car?"

Su-Na scowled. "Why must you ask so many stupid questions? We do not travel in the first-class car because we do not have the extra money."

"If a Korean had enough money to travel in the other car, would that be allowed?"

"Of course," Su-Na replied with irritation. "America is a free country. Everyone is equal. Now be quiet and let me sleep." She shut her eyes to indicate she would not speak to her sister again.

Jae-Mi waited until everyone was dozing to slip out of her seat. The air was hot and close and smelled of hair oil and fish and dust and sweat. As she used her sea legs to make her way down the lurching train car, she glanced at people's faces. Nearly every passenger had the same color hair, the same color skin that she had. At the very back of the train car she noticed a family who was different. They had black curly hair and darker faces. She checked the skin on her arm. Was she turning darker, too, since she had come to America?

When she finally reached the door separating her car from the first-class one, she took a deep breath. She wanted to see for herself. She wanted to make sure that what Su-Na had told her was true. Jae-Mi pulled on the handle of the door and to her horror discovered yet another door. And between the two doors the floor leapt and bounced with great gaps that showed the hungry track passing below. The sight was so shocking, Jae-Mi lost her grip on the first door, stumbled forward, and found herself trapped between the train cars.

Desperately, she pushed and pounded against the second door. Nothing happened. She tried again. What if she had to spend the rest of her life balanced here? She used both fists to pummel the door. She threw herself against the door. Someone had to open it. Someone had to —

Suddenly the door was flung open. She fell inside and in that instant caught a glimpse of what seemed like hundreds of astonished eyes swiveled in her direction. *Clump clump clump.* A pair of shining black shoes appeared in front of her face. She looked up. Connected to the shoes was a very tall man in a blue uniform. He seemed as enormous and powerful as the stone *miryek* from Mother's mole story. Instinctively, she shielded her head with her hands.

The *miryek* man shouted at her in English. She glanced up at him long enough to see that his distant white statue face had turned very red. This scared her even more. What if he squashed her flat? She heard someone laugh. A woman. And there was that word again. It snapped through the air like a hot slap against her cheek. "Jap!"

Jae-Mi felt someone grab her by her elbows and hoist her to her feet. The *miryek* man spoke. She couldn't understand him. She couldn't look at him. Instead she peered around his blue uniform at the passengers. Quickly, she scanned the rows. There was not one person who looked like Mother or Father, not one person who looked like anyone she knew. She felt filled with relief when the man opened both heavy doors for her and sent her back to her family.

"Where did you go?" Su-Na hissed. "You're not supposed to wander off. You know that."

Jae-Mi sat down in the hard seat. "You lied again," she said in a low voice.

"What are you talking about?" Su-Na replied. Now she really wanted to pinch her nasty sister very hard.

"There's nobody from Korea in the first-class car. Nobody." Jae-Mi shut her eyes tight so that she did not have to look at her treacherous sister. "America is not a free country. People are not equal." For the rest of their journey, Jae-Mi refused to speak to Su-Na.

When they finally arrived in Riverside, they had been traveling all day and most of the previous night. It was noontime. The heat and sunshine was so intense, the low hills and flat fields looked blasted and colorless. Waves of heat shimmered in the distance. It was impossible to see without squinting.

Father shouldered the few pieces of rolled-up bedding and the bag of clothing they had managed to take safely this far. "Here we are," he said in a cheerful voice as his family stood around him on the wooden platform at the depot. "Riverside."

Mother was holding Meung very tightly in her arms and was blinking very hard. Su-Na wondered if her eyes hurt or if she, too, was about to cry.

"I'm thirsty," Hi-Jong complained.

"Soon enough we'll find something to drink," Father said. "You wait here. I need to ask for directions." Su-Na and her sisters watched as Father approached a man in a wide-brimmed hat. This hat was so big it nearly covered the man's eyes. When father stopped the man, he pushed his hat back a little and looked Father up and down. Then he shook his head and walked on. His boots were pointy and they made a *clip-clop* noise on the wooden platform. Jai-Mi liked the sound those American boots made and she wondered if one day she might be able to try on a pair.

Father tried to talk to another man in a rounded hat who hurried past. He carried a square object with a handle. The man had a mustache like Grandfather's. His thick neck spilled over the top of his white collar. When Father finally caught his attention, the man pointed, said a few words, and kept walking.

Chagrined, Father finally returned. "I must learn English," Father mumbled. "I must learn it very soon or I will never make my way here." For a moment he seemed discouraged. But only for a moment. Quickly, he thrust his hand inside his jacket pocket and produced a piece of paper. He looked at the paper and compared it to the sign that hung over the platform.

Su-Na and her sisters crouched in the only shady spot on the platform. Su-Na surveyed the situation. She knew there was no food left in the bundle. They had no water. They had no place to sleep. They had no money. How long could they stay on this platform beside the train? What would become of them?

Someone shouted. Then another shout rang out. Jae-Mi rubbed her eyes and stared out into the bright sunlight. Someone was calling to them in Korean! The sound of that voice was so marvelous that Hi-Jong nearly burst into tears of joy. *We are saved!* Su-Na thought.

Father rushed across the platform, bowing. "Have you been in peace, venerable sir?" he asked, using the most polite form of Korean speech. The man he addressed so formally was a few years younger than he was.

Just as politely, the man exclaimed, "Yes, Uncle, and you, have you eaten your honorable meals? I am so happy you received my humble letter."

Father bowed deeply. He kept bowing. He bowed and bowed. So did Mother. Their rescuer, whose name was Mr. Paik, bowed, too. "So sorry for this delay. Please forgive me," Mr. Paik said. "We came yesterday and the day before. Always we met the wrong train. Come! Come, this way. We will give you some food. We will make you feel at home."

Su-Na and her sisters eagerly followed Mr. Paik down a dusty road that ran along the railroad tracks. They soon came upon a row of sun-beaten wooden houses that were only a short stone's throw from the train tracks. The little houses leaned against one another as if for support. "Here, here. Come in!" Mr. Paik said joyfully. He opened the door of one of the little houses and led them inside.

There was some shade inside and for a moment Su-Na and her sisters could not see. It was dark until their eyes adjusted. Su-Na blinked hard and rubbed the dust out of her eyes. When she did, she was surprised to discover that the little shack was filled with Koreans. Old and young, men and women, boys and girls. Everyone was talking and laughing. The women took Meung from Mother's arms and passed him around and muttered admiring phrases. Su-Na watched the men light pipes and tell stories. *Just like home*, she thought. And for the first time in many days, even though she knew no one in the room except Mr. Paik, she felt comfortable. She felt safe.

"Hello!" Jae-Mi said happily. She greeted each person with a respectful bow, the way she had been taught. Hi-Jong was too shy to greet anyone. She simply hid behind Mother.

Suddenly the house began to shake. Hi-Jong, convinced it was another earthquake, clutched Mother and began to scream. Jae-Mi and Su-Na looked at each other in terror. "Hush, hush," Mother said nervously as the walls trembled.

No one else acted the least bit disturbed. Mr. Paik kept talking and joking even as he reached out and held a cracked mirror hanging from a nail by a string. "Do not worry, little one," he said, and smiled at Hi-Jong. "It is only the train. Union Pacific comes through four times a day. We don't even notice anymore."

After a dinner of rice and mild *kimchee* and a few pieces of grizzled meat called salt pork, the adults began to talk in earnest. The sun slipped down near the horizon and for the first time the air began to cool. The darkening sky glittered with the first stars. Soft wind began to chant across the land. Instead of hearing the cane rustling as Su-Na was accustomed to, she heard the sound of tree leaves shaking in the wind and the smell of something sweet. Oranges and lemons. That was what Father had told them. Su-Na wondered what an orange looked like.

Shyly Su-Na and her sisters crept outside with the other children. They ranged in age from four to fourteen. None of the girls wore a *han-bok* dress. The boys had their hair cut short. None of the older children seemed the least bit embarrassed that the group was a mixture of boys and girls.

"What you name?" one of the bigger, tougher-looking girls asked Su-Na in broken Korean. She threw a ball up very high and caught it without any trouble.

"Su-Na," she replied and introduced each of her sisters, never once taking her eyes off the flying ball. The big girl's name was Minja.

"Speak English?" demanded a boy of ten who wore a ripped shirt.

Su-Na shook her head.

"Better learn," he replied, and laughed. The others laughed, too. They said something to each other in English that must have been a joke, and laughed again.

Jae-Mi's face darkened. She knew they were making fun of her and her sisters. Before she could shove Ripped Shirt Boy, Su-Na grabbed her by the arm and held her. "Let me go," Jae-Mi hissed at her eldest sister.

"No," Su-Na replied. "Remember what Father said."

Jae-Mi tried to twist free. *"Anything new and strange causes fear at first."* She scowled. *"Violence doesn't solve anything."* Remembering Father's words didn't make her feel any better. She still wanted to smash that laughing boy in the mouth, but her sister wouldn't let her go. Su-Na kept holding her until she could breathe again. But Jae-Mi's eyes flashed, "Next time. Next time, watch out!"

Meanwhile, Hi-Jong had wandered off with a girl her age. She and the little girl were arranging pebbles on a flat board. "We saw an earthquake," Hi-Jong bragged.

The little girl, who knew Korean better than English, looked at her with astonishment. "What happened? Did you get hurt?"

Hi-Jong gave the girl a sideways glance. She could tell the girl was impressed. "The ground swallowed me and my family. Then *spit!* We flew out. We were safe. What's your name?"

"Emily. What's your name?"

Hi-Jong poked her toe in the dirt. She stared at the hole she made and wondered if she might be able to make an earthquake just by talking about it. "Hi-Jong is my name."

Emily giggled. "Funny name."

Hi-Jong bit her lips between her teeth. She held very still and blinked hard. She did not want to cry. Not here. Not in front of this girl who might be her friend.

Emily stopped giggling. "That's an earthquake name, right?"

"Right," said Hi-Jong, brightening.

That evening Su-Na and her sisters followed their parents down the dirt path to their new home. Father carried Meung in his arms. He was in such a good mood, he was humming. They passed a few water pumps and two small houses that made the girls hold their noses. "Outhouses," Father said simply. "Remember where they are."

Su-Na and her sisters wanted to forget where they were. They smelled horrible. Finally they came to their new home. Mr. Paik had told Father that these wooden, one-room shacks were built by Chinese men who had worked for the Southern Pacific Railroad. This was where they had lived. Because the shacks were old and wooden, the dry climate had shrunk the boards. Wind blew through the cracks.

"We will put mud in the cracks to keep out the wind," Father said, inspecting the walls. His old take-charge voice had returned. He seemed energized and ready for anything.

"Where will we take baths?" asked Mother.

"We will heat bath water in a bucket over an open

fire outside," Father said, "then pour it into a tin tub inside."

"What about light?" Jae-Mi asked. It seemed dark and spooky in the shack. What if some old Chinese ghost were watching her right at this very moment?

"Kerosene lanterns," Father said. "We'll try to borrow one tomorrow. Su-Na, your job will be to trim the wicks, clean the glass tops, and keep the bowls filled with kerosene."

"Why not Jae-Mi?" Su-Na grumbled. "She's the one who asked."

"What?" Father demanded.

"Nothing, sir," Su-Na replied meekly. She and her sisters fell quickly asleep on pallets borrowed from Mr. Paik.

The next morning Su-Na and her sisters woke up early and discovered that Father was already working. After long discussions with Mother and several of the other Korean men, he had agreed to a plan for Mother to work. They would open a dining hall for the thirty Korean bachelors who worked in the nearby citrus groves.

Clearly, Father was not completely pleased with idea that Mother would work outside the house, but he had no choice. Somehow they had to make a living. What was even more humiliating for him, however, was that he had to go to the Chinese settlement and beg to borrow cooking utensils and food to begin their business. Since Father did not speak Chinese and the Chinese store owner did not speak Korean, they communicated using one thing they both knew: *hanmum*, a special kind of script.

When Father reappeared back at the house with big iron pots and pans, dishes, tin lunch pails, chopsticks, and bags of rice and other groceries, he was pleased to report that the Chinese grocer was quite a scholar even though he was Chinese.

"You must help me," Mother told Su-Na and her sisters. "We will cook breakfast at five A.M., pack lunches, and then cook supper at seven P.M. Plus I will need help watching Meung so that he does not crawl into the fire."

"But where will the men eat?" Jae-Mi asked. "Our one-room house is much too small to serve thirty people."

Mother laughed. "Wait and see."

Outside, Father, Mr. Paik, and a few others were noisily hammering and sawing. They had just returned from the dumpyard with pieces of board and barrels and rusty pieces of metal. The men built a new shack large enough for the dining area, which they furnished with handmade benches and two long tables made from sawhorses and old doors. Father created a large stove and oven using mud and straw. He dragged four empty wine barrels from the dump to hold drinking and cooking water.

Even though Su-Na thought the new dining hall

was anything but elegant-looking, the people in the settlement beside the railroad tracks seemed delighted. It would be the first time that many of the homesick single men could get a good, hot Korean meal.

When they were finished fixing up the dining area and equipping the kitchen, Father went to work on improving the house. With extra wood from the dump, he built shelves along the four walls of the shack for child-size beds. He found hay for each shelf, put a blanket over this, and rolled up old clothes for a pillow. He and Mother slept on the floor.

Su-Na and her sisters soon discovered that there was more than enough work to do to keep the restaurant running. Every morning they had to wake up early and gather wood from the dump and in the scrubby woods nearby. They had to make sure there was enough water in the water barrels. Jae-Mi had to take care of Meung while Mother cooked breakfast. Hi-Jong and Su-Na helped fill the buckets with bath water for the men so that they could take a bath at six o'clock every night when they returned from picking in the hot, dusty citrus groves.

On the first day the dining hall opened for business there were more customers than plates, more plates than food. Mother, who was an excellent cook, had never prepared a meal for so many people at once. She scrambled around cooking more rice, more fried salt pork. The heat was intense inside the windowless shack, so they kept the door open. Flies swarmed. Hi-Jong's job was to watch her brother and wave a piece of stiff paper in the air to keep the flies off the food.

As soon as the men ate, they grabbed the lunch pails Mother had packed with rice and *kimchee* and disappeared into the groves. Father, who had signed on as a fruit picker, went along. After the first breakfast, Mother appeared to be exhausted. Next came another several hours of cleaning. Su-Na and her sisters helped wash the dishes in a huge tub set on a bench outside the dining room shack.

When every last plate and chopstick was cleaned, Su-Na came back inside. "What are you doing?" she asked Mother in horror.

Mother stood before a small broken mirror Father had nailed to the wall above the hand basin. She had a dull pair of scissors in her hand and she was cutting her long, beautiful hair. Long strands fell around her feet. Su-Na was too stunned to speak.

"My hair is in my way," Mother said. "We are in America now. I need to look like an American."

Su-Na shook her head. When Jae-Mi and Hi-Jong came into the dining room and saw Mother's hair on the floor they were equally shocked. "It looks like a dead animal," Hi-Jong said, staring at the heap of hair.

"What will Father say?" Jae-Mi said.

That evening when Father came home, he noticed

immediately what Mother had done. He was enraged. "Why? Why must you insult me like this?" he demanded. "Is it not bad enough to have my wife work? Now this. What would the ancestors say? This is an ancient custom, your hair—"

"You cut your topknot."

"That was different."

"Was it?" Mother asked, then paused. "We have already lost everything else that means anything to us. Losing my hair does not disturb me. Besides, it is a nuisance while I cook. Now, enough. There is work to do. Go and help carry water. It is far too heavy for the girls."

Chagrined, Father did as he was told. Su-Na watched, amazed. Never before had Mother openly disobeyed Father. Su-Na waited for some catastrophe, some terrible sign—lightning from the sky, another earthquake. But nothing big and obvious happened. What occurred was far more subtle and difficult to trace over time. As days and months passed and the dining business thrived, Su-Na and her sisters became aware that their mother seemed to grow imperceptibly taller. Perhaps it was because Father had begun to shrink.

Chapter

7

My father's hope springs like
blossom sprouts from dead branches
at winter's end.
What sun shines on him so that he
never gives up?
No one else seems to notice
the change in season.

Days passed. Mother was so busy cooking and cleaning and running the dining hall that she did not have
time to sing about Ariray Hill or tell stories about
dragon children or share memories of growing up in
Korea so long ago that people walked on high wooden
shoes to keep their feet out of the mud. With every
passing month, the girls' memories of Korea began to
fade. They soon began to confuse what happened dur-

ing their year in Hawaii with what happened when they still lived in Seoul.

Father, who worked from dawn to dusk in the fields picking oranges and lemons, came home so exhausted that he, too, had no energy to talk. Su-Na missed sharing *sijo* poems with him. Grandmother had taught Su-Na how to read using the Korean *hangul* alphabet that she herself had learned from the missionaries. So few people in the settlement knew how to read this form of writing, Su-Na considered it her own special code. Even if she had no one with whom to share them, Su-Na wrote her secret poems on scraps of paper. This helped her feel less lonely.

Although Father was too busy to discuss poetry, he always had time to talk about their family's glorious future. And part of the glorious future that he imagined had to do with his children going to school and succeeding as scholars. School was very important to Su-Na's parents. One day Father announced that all three girls would be going in September to Washington Irving School not far from the settlement. Mr. Paik, who knew some English, had promised to take them. September seemed very far away and the girls did not think any more of it. They had so much to do helping Mother that they could not imagine that September would ever arrive.

Of all their chores, the one Su-Na hated most happened every Saturday morning. That was the day that

she and her sisters walked across town to the slaughterhouse to collect the animal organs that the butchers
threw out as garbage. These were the pork and beef
livers, the hearts, kidneys, and entrails that were not
wanted.

"Do we have to go?" Jae-Mi asked. She lingered
outside their small house with her two sisters on
Saturday morning. She had plans to finish her chores
and then build a kite.

Hi-Jong was particularly squeamish near the building. The cries of the animals and the stench was too
horrible. "I would rather stay home."

"Mother said you have to help. How else can I carry
the sacks? Come on and stop making excuses," Su-Na
replied.

Reluctantly, each of her sisters picked up a burlap
feed sack. They knew what happened if they complained to Father. He would only say the same thing
he said every time. "We should thank God that the
butchers don't know the value of what they throw out,
otherwise we would go hungry." The girls trudged
reluctantly along the railroad tracks toward the other
side of town. Su-Na did not need to mention her
father's rule. "Do not go alone into town. Always
travel together. If anything should happen, one of you
can help the other."

A tumbleweed blew across the track. A lonesome
horn sounded. The girls stepped off the track. Right

on schedule, the train roared past. Dust and grit flew. The girls shielded their eyes. Father always said the same thing every time the train passed through: "I wonder why the Chinese loved that train so much that they had to build their houses nearly on top of the track?"

Of course, Su-Na knew he was joking. She was pretty sure they didn't have a choice where they built their houses. And she also knew that Father did not dislike all Chinese. Hadn't he been pleased to borrow most of the equipment and dishes they needed to start up the dining hall from a Chinese man?

Even so, this whole issue of people and language and skin color perplexed Su-Na. As they walked along through the Korean settlement they came to the Chinese settlement and then past that they walked through the few houses owned by the Japanese and finally they came to the Mexican settlement. All these houses were outside Riverside. "Why do you suppose the Koreans, Chinese, Japanese, and Mexicans all live here outside town?" Hi-Jong asked Su-Na.

Su-Na shrugged. When she had asked Father the same question, he had answered, "Ignorance." This did not help her because that was all he said. Who was ignorant? He never explained.

"If we were all equal, we could live together," Jae-Mi said. She tossed a rock across the track. "The problem is that some people always think they're better."

"Better than what?" Hi-Jong asked. None of this made sense to her. Absentmindedly, she picked up a rusty can for Gold Stone peaches. On the can was a colorful label with a smiling blond child. "Can you change your skin color?"

"Of course not," Su-Na said. "Only God can decide what color you are."

"Who told you that?" Jae-Mi demanded.

"Father," Su-Na replied.

Hi-Jong kicked the empty can and watched it bounce. "I would like to be a different color sometimes. And I would like to change my hair, too. I would like to have curly red hair like that little girl in the depot."

"What girl?" Jae-Mi asked and rolled her eyes.

"She had curly red hair and she rushed right past. That's all I saw," Hi-Jong said. "She had a happy face."

"Can we please hurry?" Su-Na insisted. It was only eight o'clock in the morning, but she wanted to be first to the slaughterhouse. Town was still empty. But if the girls took too long, they'd have to walk back when it was busy and then people would see them carrying the bags and they might make fun of them. The people might say something. Sometimes the bags dripped and sometimes stray dogs followed them and people laughed. Su-Na sighed and wished she were invisible.

When they finally reached the slaughterhouse they saw that they were not the first arrivals. Gathered together was another small group of a half dozen children about their age. Like Su-Na and her sisters, they carried an assortment of bags. The children eyed the sisters suspiciously and spoke words that the girls did not understand. "Don't say anything to them," warned Su-Na, who did not even recognize the language they were speaking. Was it Portuguese? Was it Spanish? Perhaps they were from the Philippines. She couldn't be sure.

"Why shouldn't we talk to them?" Jae-Mi asked. "They're here for the same reason we are."

" 'If you try to make friends with a tiger you will end up in his stomach,' " Su-Na replied.

Hi-Jong laughed. "They aren't tigers. They are children."

Su-Na blushed. She had thought the same thing when Father told her that saying.

The door swung open and the butcher with the bloody apron appeared. He carried a bucket in each hand. He placed one on the doorstep and did not look up. Certainly he knew the children were there. But he did not acknowledge them. He lifted one bucket at a time and dumped it on a concrete slab, turned, and went back inside for two more buckets to dump into the garbage heap.

As soon as he disappeared, Su-Na and her sisters and the other children dashed to the spot and scrambled for choice pieces. They frantically dug through the bloody pile for kidneys and livers. Their hands were red with blood. Their elbows were red. They stuffed the pieces into their bags. Suddenly they heard the sound of laughter. Two butchers smoking cigarettes stood in the doorway and watched, laughing.

A Mexican girl a little older than Su-Na looked up at the men and said under her breath, *"Puerco."*

In that instant, Jae-Mi looked up, too. The girls' defiant eyes met. *"Puerco,"* Jae-Mi repeated. She didn't know what the word meant but she liked the satisfying sound of it. The word seemed to describe the men who were making fun of them perfectly. For a split second, the two girls felt united in that much: their disdain of being made fun of. *"Puerco,"* she said again.

The Mexican children smiled as if they were surprised to hear this Korean girl speaking their language. One of them tossed a kidney to Jae-Mi that she had not seen. Jae-Mi stuffed it into the bag, and nodded her thanks.

Su-Na watched all this in her usual aloof manner. She did not speak or smile, she only observed. She observed how the eldest Mexican girl struggled to keep the younger children from fighting. Maybe she and that girl were not so different, Su-Na thought. Su-Na was responsible for her sisters, too. They were all hungry. And they were all trying to find something for their families to eat.

The door slammed and the men went back inside. The show was over for the day. Su-Na motioned for her sisters to wipe their hands on a rag she had brought along. She did not want them walking through town looking so filthy.

The Mexican children watched the girls. Su-Na handed the rag to the girl her age. The girl said, *"Gracias."* She wiped her hands and made her reluctant companions do the same, then gave the rag back to Su-Na.

"Gracias," Su-Na said bravely. If Jae-Mi could speak Spanish, why couldn't she? Su-Na tied the rag to a string on the bag for the next visit. The children went their separate ways.

"What did you say about tigers?" Hi-Jong said as they started walking home again.

"Nothing," Su-Na replied.

Without warning, summer ended. It was September, the dreaded month when school began. One morning Mother and Father went over the rules for their behavior in great detail. "Respect your teacher. Do not fight. Be generous. Do not say any words that will bring discord upon the classroom. Be clean and courteous at all times," Father said.

"Yes, yes," Su-Na replied. She was wearing her only dress, which Mother had washed. Her sisters' hair had been neatly combed and braided. They had a lunch pail to share, with rice balls wrapped in newspaper. Everything was ready. Su-Na felt as if she might throw up.

"Do we have to go?" Hi-Jong asked, her voice trembling.

"School is a privilege. You must do your best. Your very best," Father replied. "It is a great sacrifice to send you and you must bring honor to your family."

Mr. Paik arrived to walk the girls to school, which was on the other side of town. They had never walked in this neighborhood before. There were trees and gardens and flowers that reminded Hi-Jong of Hawaii. She was amazed to see so many large, beautiful homes. Su-Na followed with her eyes downcast, terrified to look at the Riverside residents who were watching them from their porches. Jae-Mi felt as if she were going to her own execution. Every so often she shot a glance in all directions to see where they were going. She had to memorize the route. Perhaps she would run away —

"Here we are," Mr. Paik announced. They turned the corner and heard the sound of children shouting and laughing on the playground. Boys ran and threw balls. Girls swung ropes and played hopscotch with pebbles. Only a half dozen at the most looked as if they might be from Korea, Japan, or China.

"Now be good." He turned to leave.

"I thought . . . I thought you were coming in, sir," Su-Na said in panic. *Don't leave us.*

"Everything is arranged. I have already spoken to the principal. She is eager to meet you," Mr. Paik said.

"Just go in and tell the teacher your names." He disappeared down the sidewalk.

The playground on the other side of the fence was vast and crowded. Beyond the playground was a tall brick building with glass windows. There was something foreboding about that building, Su-Na decided. It looked so big. What if they went inside and became lost?

"I want to go home," Hi-Jong whispered. The children looked enormous. She did not see anyone her age. She did not see any Korean children. What if these children did not like her?

With interest Jae-Mi studied a game. The boys hit a ball with a stick and then ran. It looked like a very interesting game. "Maybe we can just stay for a little while. I want to see what happens." She wandered past the fence and onto the playground.

Su-Na, who knew she was responsible for her sister's safety, followed her. "Come back," Su-Na called, dragging Hi-Jong onto the playground by her hand.

Before they had gone even a few more steps, Su-Na and her sisters were surrounded by more white children than they had ever seen in their lives. The American girls formed a ring around Su-Na and her sisters and sang words in English that Su-Na did not understand. What were they saying? What did they want? Was this some kind of welcome? Their faces were fearfully pale. Some of them had fuzzy hair and nearly colorless eyes.

Without warning, the girls who danced around them suddenly stopped. One of the girls, smiling broadly, rushed forward toward Su-Na and with a chopping motion hit her in the neck with her hand. Su-Na stumbled backward in disbelief. She shielded her head and tried to escape but the girl did not stop. She kept chopping while the other girls laughed and laughed.

Hi-Jong and Jae-Mi rushed away. "Come on!" Jae-Mi shouted in Su-Na's direction. "Run!"

But Su-Na could not escape. She bent nearly double and stumbled. Jae-Mi pushed up her sleeves and charged back into the crowd with her head down. She tackled two girls then grabbed the stunned neck-chopper by the waist. She clamped her arms around the girl's waist and pulled her away from Su-Na with the ferocity of a bulldog. "Leave her alone, white devil!" she screamed in Korean. She would kill this girl if she did not leave her sister alone.

"Jae-Mi!" Su-Na shouted.

But Jae-Mi would not let go. She was determined to make sure her sister was safe. The shrieking neck-chopper twisted and turned. Her arms windmilled. But she could not free herself from Jae-Mi.

"Get out of here!" Jae-Mi called to Su-Na. The neck-chopper dragged Jae-Mi a few feet, lost her balance, and fell over. Her dress was torn. Her knee was bloody.

The crowd of children gasped and started shouting.

Someone screamed. And then all was silent as the crowd parted. A terrifying woman with bright yellow hair and big blue eyes stared down at Jae-Mi. Su-Na tried to speak to her and bowed repeatedly. The woman with the terrifying hair kept talking. She spoke to several of the children from the crowd. Her mouth frowned. She pointed at the children and motioned for them to do something.

"I don't understand," Su-Na kept saying in Korean. She was crying now. It was horribly humiliating to have so many people watching her. She wanted to fall into a hole and vanish.

Jae-Mi watched the defeated neck-chopper saunter away. The girl looked over her shoulder at Jae-Mi and made one last threatening motion with her hands.

The woman with the terrifying hair bent over so that she could look directly into Jae-Mi's eyes. This was the most horrible experience of all. The woman's eyes were the color of melting ice. Jae-Mi, absolutely terrified by being so close for so long to a white grown-up, turned, grabbed Hi-Jong, who was sobbing, and bolted off the playground at full speed.

Su-Na was not as quick. She was stopped by the woman, who held her arm gently and led her into the brick building. The woman kindly handed Su-Na the lunch pail. But Su-Na could think of nothing to say, nothing to do. She was too scared. This woman was taking her to the place where the chopping children had gone. Certainly she would not survive. She was only glad that her sisters had escaped. Of course, Father and Mother would be angry. They would be disappointed. But at least they'd still have two surviving daughters, even though they had broken all the rules Father had set. They had brought dishonor to the family.

The woman led Su-Na up a flight of stairs into the brick building that had a strange smell. Su-Na was reminded of the closed-up smell of ancestors' crypts back in Korea and something sweet and putrid like decaying meat. She sniffed. Paper. She was also smelling paper. She sighed, thinking how fine it would be to have plenty of paper to write poems. Well, it was too late now for such idle dreams. Certainly she was going to be locked up. Perhaps in a jail.

She walked along a long hallway with a shining, slippery floor. Whenever they passed a door, she looked in and saw many white faces. There were children sitting on little chairs. Bigger children sat on bigger chairs. They stared at her in a frankly curious, pitying way as if to say, "Too bad for you."

Su-Na gulped. When they reached the end of the forever long hallway they came to a room with grown-ups. Like the woman with terrifying hair, these women all had bright white faces. A few had brown hair. One had black hair. They looked at Su-Na and they did not smile. Were they the jailers?

The woman with the terrifying hair motioned for Su-

Na to sit in a chair with a soft seat. Su-Na folded her hands in her lap. Her palms sweated. The chair made a squeaking noise whenever she moved. She wondered if that was part of the trick. If she broke the chair, what would she say? Would she have to stay in jail longer?

The woman kept smiling at Su-Na. She had very fine white teeth the color of porcelain. She blinked many times. Su-Na watched the woman put glasses on. The glasses made her look like a different person. Su-Na wondered if now she would be the angry woman with terrifying hair. But no. She kept talking to Su-Na in a gentle murmur that made no sense.

"I don't understand you," Su-Na kept saying in Korean. "I don't understand you."

The woman wrote something that Su-Na could not read on a piece of paper. She stood up and motioned for Su-Na to follow her. *Now I am surely going to be locked up,* Su-Na thought. *I wonder if this woman will ever tell my parents where I am.*

They retraced their steps down the slippery hallway. But instead of taking Su-Na to a jail with bars, they entered one of the rooms with the many children. The woman rapped on the door frame with her knuckle. Immediately, the other woman in the room looked up. Tiny, dusty glasses perched on her snub nose. Her gray hair was gathered on the top of her head so tightly that her eyes looked squinty. She, too, did not smile when she saw Su-Na.

The woman with the tiny glasses pointed to a chair and a table in the back of the room. Su-Na shuffled in that direction, conscious of a hundred eyes bearing down on her. She wished she could vanish. She wished she could simply melt away. Slowly, she lowered herself onto the chair. For the rest of the morning, she sat there, listening to a language she did not understand. The woman moved back and forth in front of the room. Sometimes she drew on the black surface with a squawking piece of white rock. Sometimes she pointed to a book she was holding with her hand. The children's voices made a singsong noise as they read aloud. The dull, lulling sound made Su-Na sleepy. She leaned her elbow on the table and put her head in her hand. She tried very hard to pay attention. She tried—

A bell rang someplace. The sound shocked Su-Na into wakefulness. She sat up rigid, alert, and ready for more torture. The other children leapt to their feet even as the woman with the tiny glasses called to them. They did not bow to her. They did not look at her. They simply rushed out of the room. The woman watched with helpless disapproval on her skinny face.

Su-Na stood, unsure what to do next. There was only one other girl in the classroom. When the girl turned, Su-Na was surprised to see that it was the older Mexican girl from the slaughterhouse. *Is she in trouble, too?* Su-Na tried to think of something to say.

But what? They did not speak the same language. *Should I smile? Should I wave?*

The girl turned. *Surely she recognizes me.* But the girl looked right through Su-Na as if she were not even there. Helplessly, Su-Na watched her shuffle out of the room.

Chapter

8

I am invisible because people
refuse to see me.
When they come close they
peer into a broken mirror.
My surroundings, themselves, or
their imaginings—
they spy everything but me.

Su-Na returned home from her first endless day of
school filled with dread. Not until she left the brick
building and began trudging back did she begin to
wonder where her sisters might have gone. She
assumed they had run home. What if they had become
lost? Surely Mother would blame her. And then there
would be one more problem to blame on her. Not only
had she dishonored her family, she had not met her

responsibilities to her sisters. She could deal with Mother now, perhaps. What she dreaded most was Father when he came home from work. What would she tell him? How would she explain her terrible failure?

Slowly, she pushed the door open. She heard voices. To her amazement and horror, Mother *and* Father sat motionless on the low bench, their heads in their hands. Her Mother was always in motion, always busy—cleaning or cooking or taking care of Meung. Why was she so still? What had happened? And what was Father doing home so soon?

Cold dread gripped Su-Na. *It's worse than what I imagined.* She gulped and took a step forward. In one of the beds something wiggled. It was Meung lying on his back, waving his hands in the air. There was no sign of her sisters. An open Korean newspaper was spread on the floor in front of her parents. Su-Na bowed respectfully. "Mother, Father, I—"

Her parents looked up at her with startled, sorrowful eyes. They did not speak. They did not reprimand her.

"What happened?" Su-Na asked in a small voice.

"Mr. Paik gave us this newspaper. It says churches are burned in our country. Schools are closed. Innocent people are put in jail. Things are very bad in Korea now because of the Japanese. They have taken over the government, the military, everything," Father said. "I fear for our people."

"And Grandmother? What about Grandfather?"

Su-Na asked anxiously. "And our other relatives left behind?"

Mother glanced hurriedly at Father. "We will have to hope and pray for the best. When we see them again . . ." Her voice trailed off. She dabbed her eyes with her sleeve.

"We don't know when we will return. We cannot think that way now. Please, please calm yourself—"

Su-Na quietly withdrew. There was something awful happening. What could she do? Miserably, she trudged outside. Korea seemed very far away. She felt distressed about her grandparents' safety. But she was also worried about her own situation. Her parents did not mention school or her sisters. What would they do when they found out about the disastrous day at school?

Suddenly she heard familiar voices. "Hi-Jong?" Su-Na called softly. What had her sisters told them? "Jae-Mi?"

"Over here."

Su-Na looked up and saw her two sisters huddled on the roof of one of the abandoned sheds. "What are you doing up there?"

"What does it look like?" Jae-Mi waved for Su-Na to join them. "We're hiding." Jae-Mi's sleeve was torn and her face was still dirty from the fight on the playground. Hi-Jong looked equally terrified.

"Have you been here all day? Do Mother and

Father know where you are?" Su-Na demanded. She stood on the ground, her fists at her waist, and looked up at her gloomy-faced sisters. "Cowards."

"Who are you calling cowards?" Jae-Mi replied angrily. She began to scramble down but suddenly thought better of the idea and stayed where she was. What if Father caught her?

"They will find out soon enough. Come down now if you know what's good for you," Su-Na said. They could not stay on the roof forever. Besides, she did not want to suffer her punishment alone.

"Girls!" Father called.

"See?" Su-Na said wisely. She watched her trembling sisters scramble off the roof. There was no escape now.

Father stood near the pump, splashing water on his face. He ran his hand through his thick hair. "I want to talk to you."

The girls trudged closer. They stood staring at their battered shoes. They twisted pleats of skirt between their fingers. "How was your first day of school?"

Su-Na gulped. As eldest she decided it was her responsibility to tell him what had happened. "It was terrible, Father."

"Evil girls tried to chop off Su-Na's head," Hi-Jong interrupted.

Jae-Mi nodded. "I could not let her be killed."

And then all three sisters began talking all at once.

". . . The white woman talked and talked . . ."

". . . And Jae-Mi held tight like a tiger . . ."

". . . Didn't understand a word . . ."

". . . We ran away because . . ."

". . . I sat all day. No one spoke to me . . ."

". . . We were too scared . . ."

". . . Don't make us go back, Father . . ."

". . . Please, Father, please . . ."

Father's mouth had a stern expression. A bad sign. Su-Na held her breath. Now for the punishment. Now for the terrible ending to a terrible day.

"There is nothing to be afraid of," he said slowly. "Now that we are living in America, where everything is different from Korea, we must learn to get along with everyone. We are the lucky ones. We are in a place where life is better. Do you understand?"

"But, Father . . ." Su-Na pleaded. She did not understand. *Lucky?* She did not feel the least bit lucky.

"Tomorrow you will go back," Father said. "You will try again. And you will do this to bring honor to your family."

Su-Na and her sisters bowed and did not argue. They knew it was pointless.

The next morning the girls retraced their footsteps to Washington Irving School, certain that they would meet their doom. Su-Na tried to look brave. She tried to encourage Hi-Jong. She tried to convince Jae-Mi not to slug the first person who jumped them. "Maybe today will be better," Su-Na said, although she did not feel hopeful.

Amazingly enough, although the same girls twirled around on the pavement and the same boys tossed balls into the air, no ring of nasty neck-choppers encircled them. The sisters walked across the playground untouched. No one spoke to them. No one greeted them. No one asked their names. But no one hurt them.

"Must you hold my hand so tightly?" Su-Na complained when she finally wrenched Hi-Jong's fingers free. The little girl immediately began to whimper. Jae-Mi scowled to have to stand so close to her youngest, weeping sister. What would the other children think? "I survived yesterday," Su-Na whispered to her sisters. "You will survive, too."

"How?" Hi-Jong begged desperately.

Jae-Mi bit her fingernails. "I think this is a big mistake."

"Don't make a fuss. Don't fight. Get along with everyone, just as Father said," Su-Na hurriedly advised her middle sister. Then she turned to Hi-Jong. "Do not act like a baby. Be invisible. That's the trick."

"Invisible? How?" Hi-Jong said, and groaned.

Before Su-Na could answer, the bell rang. The children dashed and pushed and shouted toward the door. They lined up in fidgeting rows. And in just a few moments the great dark brick building swallowed all the children, including Su-Na and her sisters.

Little by little, week by week, the girls grew accustomed to the routine of getting up very early in the morning to help their mother prepare the fire and draw water for the dining hall breakfast. They grew accustomed to going to school and then returning home at the end of the day to help prepare the dinner meal.

Meanwhile at school Su-Na and her sisters experienced a never-ending parade of meaningless, confounding holidays. The first celebrations were called Halloween and Thanksgiving. They wore silly cutout cardboard hats shaped like cones and they sang songs with cheery words they did not understand. "Tur-KEY. Tur-KEY!" When Christmas came, they were relegated to the roles of sheep and oxen in the school's Christmas pageant. In February, Su-Na and her sisters cut many hearts from pieces of beautiful red paper and copied many names onto the hearts, but no one sent them any in return.

By the time spring came again, Su-Na had discovered that she was very good at fading into the walls, the playground fence, the auditorium curtain—anything handy that would make her seem as unnoticeable as possible. She was always courteous in class. She nodded her head and acted as if she understood the incomprehensible things the teacher and the other children were saying. She never spoke if she could help it. To be invisible meant that no one would pick on her, she decided. She learned to walk like white children, dress like white children, talk like white children. She even learned to eat like white children. She practiced eating without showing enjoyment. She sipped her soup without making noise. She did not open her mouth with food in it. She used a fork, chewed with her lips closed, and did not smack her lips to signal she was full. None of these things came easily. This was not how she was taught to eat in Korea.

As for Jae-Mi, she soon earned a reputation that protected her from attack. Not even the boys in her class dared make fun of her because she was such a fierce fighter. Girls avoided her. She kept mostly to herself. Hi-Jong, on the other hand, seemed to enjoy going to school. She picked up English quickly because she found several little girls in her class who weren't afraid to talk to her. She liked to comb their hair, which was long and soft and the color of straw. The girls did not mind.

One day at recess on the first pleasant day of spring, the children milled about outdoors in the sunshine. Su-Na leaned against the fence and pretended to be studying the sky. She found that if she always seemed busy doing something that required only one person, no one would bother her. She scowled studiously at clouds floating past. To while away the endless recess, she composed a forlorn poem in her head:

To be a cloud, speechless
is very lonely.
No one sees me watching overhead.
I float and leave no trace.
Sometimes I wonder if I am real.

Every so often she glanced toward Hi-Jong, who was swinging on the large swing set. Across the way Jae-Mi tossed a ball in the air. Her sisters did not appear to feel as hopeless as she did.

Suddenly from the other side of the playground came the sound of voices and the chilling memory of a song. Su-Na shielded her eyes and gazed at the same group of older girls who had greeted her with a neck-chop on the first day of school. Jae-Mi and Hi-Jong seemed to remember the song, too. They drifted closer to Su-Na, as if for protection.

"What is going on?" Su-Na whispered in Korean.

"New students," Jae-Mi said. She watched two black-haired boys and a girl cautiously cross the fence line into dangerous territory. The boys looked about eight or nine years old, the girl slightly younger. She was very thin and walked between them. One boy twisted his hat in his hands. The other carried a lunch pail clutched to his chest.

"Chinese?" Hi-Jong asked, staring.

"No, Japanese," Su-Na replied. She could tell from the calligraphy painted on their lunch pail.

Immediately, the other girls ringed the three new-comers and began singing the chant over and over. "What are they saying?" Su-Na demanded. "I cannot understand all the words."

Hi-Jong translated:

"Ching Chong, Chinaman,
Sitting on a wall.
Along came a white man,
And chopped his head off."

Then, just as before, one of the girls stepped forward and gave all three terrified children a "chop" on the neck with the side of her hand. The crowd cheered and laughed.

Su-Na watched, appalled. *So that's what that song meant.* "We should do something. We should help them."

"Not me," Hi-Jong said. "I don't want to get in trouble again."

The three children stumbled toward the school door in terror. The little girl's eyes streamed with tears. The two boys tried to appear brave. When they glanced in the direction of Su-Na and her sisters, none of the girls did anything to help. They did not wave. They did not say hello. They looked at the three new-comers as if they were invisible.

"Japs," Jae-Mi muttered.

"Glad it's them, not us," Hi-Jong said quietly to no one in particular.

"But what if it was us?" Su-Na exploded in anger. How could her sisters stand there and say such awful words? They knew what it felt like to be surrounded and made fun of. Why didn't they act, now that they knew what that awful chant meant? *Along came a white man and chopped his head off.*

"Aren't they the enemy? Isn't that what Father said?" Hi-Jong said. "Japanese deserve to be chopped."

"I don't see you doing anything heroic, Su-Na," Jae-Mi said with a sneer. "You'd rather not get involved. 'Stay invisible,' isn't that your motto?"

Su-Na felt her face flush bright red. Of course her sisters were right. She shouldn't be the one to talk about helping other people. In silence she watched as the crowd resumed baseball and hopscotch and jump rope. It was almost as if the three strangers had never been there.

"Hey, you!" someone shouted.

Su-Na turned and saw a girl with long yellow hair motioning toward Hi-Jong. "Is that your name now?" Jae-Mi asked, chuckling.

"Very funny," Hi-Jong replied and waved. "No one can remember my name. That's why I'm changing it. I told my teacher my name is Margaret. It sounds more American." Without another word, Hi-Jong skipped across the playground to play with the other girl.

Wistfully, Su-Na watched her sister. "Maybe that's the trick. A new name," she said quietly.

Jae-Mi shrugged. "I don't think Mother or Father would like it if we changed our names."

"Father said everything is different here. We have to learn to get along with everyone," Su-Na replied. She kept a watchful eye on where the neck-chopping girls were at all times. Perhaps it couldn't hurt to have a name someone could say. It might be a kind of protection. "Susan. How does that sound?"

"Sounds like Su-Na, only backward," Jae-Mi replied thoughtfully. "I'd pick a fierce, scary-sounding name if I were you. If you sound tough, the other students will leave you alone. What about Spike or Lionkiller or Snakestrangler?"

"Ridiculous," Su-Na replied. "Those aren't proper American girls' names."

Jae-Mi shrugged. "I like them all the same."

Below me the river is deep
Behind me orange trees as far as I can see.
Wind stirs, dust stings my eyes
and I miss the beauty.
Only at night under the stars
can I forget so many troubles.

Mother's dining hall business never lacked for customers. The homesick Korean bachelors loyally
crowded in every dawn and every evening for a fresh,
hot meal of *kimchee* and rice. They spoke with longing
voices about old favorites like *kalbi* and *kaktugui kimchee*, short ribs and turnip squares, *kwae chorin* and
tabu, blue crabs in soy sauce and bean curd.

Soon there were so many diners that Mother suggested they build an addition on the original dining

area. Father and a few of his friends found some lumber and expanded the space to fit another long table. When a second boy was born, named Edward to be as American as possible, Father was delighted. He declared Edward an auspicious sign for the family's improving fortune.

The new baby meant more work for Su-Na and her sisters. They had to take care of Edward and Meung, just twenty-months old, and finish their other duties before they left for school in the morning.

When the girls complained, Father reminded them how hard everyone worked following the crops from field to orchard. "If you pick grapes you risk being stung by black widow spiders and yellow jacket hornets in the vines," Father said. "Peaches must be dusted with a feather to knock off the bugs and the fuzz makes you itch like crazy by the end of the day."

He explained how hot and breathless the fields became. At dawn the temperature in the warmer months might already be eighty degrees. By noon the thermometer easily reached one hundred and ten. Without any breeze, Father and the other workers searched out a shady place to eat their lunches. When the orange season ended, there were lemons and grapefruit to pick. And when that ended, there were the walnut groves.

While Su-Na and her sisters were glad that they did not have to pick fruit or vegetables, they still felt sorry for themselves. Since they had left Hawaii and come to California, there was little time for play. Jae-Mi's most despised chore was washing the lunch buckets every day and setting them out to dry so that Mother could refill them later with food for the next day's lunches.

During orange-picking season, Jae-Mi was feeling particularly sorry for herself. Partly out of curiosity and partly to prove that she worked very hard, too, she asked one of Mother's customers why he never brought her an orange. "I have never tasted one, you know," she told the friendly Uncle.

The next day several of the empty lunch pails seemed unusually heavy. She was surprised to discover when she opened them that three of the pails contained a beautiful orange. She gave one to each of her sisters and kept one for herself. The girls sat on the roof of the old shed and carefully peeled the oranges' thick skins and enjoyed every last sweet bite.

"Does Father know about these oranges?" Su-Na asked suspiciously.

Jae-Mi shook her head and tried to look innocent. "I don't know who gave them to me. It's a mystery." This was partly true, since the second and third oranges were surprises.

The next day she was surprised to discover three more oranges. Again Jae-Mi excitedly shared the fruit with her sisters. She saved her orange and carefully brought it to school to eat for lunch. An orange was a great luxury and she knew it. The other children who sat outside on the shady side of the building watched Jae-Mi carefully as she peeled the orange. Some licked their lips.

The only girl who did not seem fascinated by Jae-Mi's orange was Kyoko, the newest girl who had come with her two brothers a few months earlier. She always sat apart and ate alone. She did not look up. She did not even glance in Jae-Mi's direction. This lack of interest in Jae-Mi's treasure infuriated Jae-Mi. She decided she must do something. Boldly, she crossed the playground, sat beside Kyoko, and offered her a section of the orange.

Kyoko looked up, surprised, but she readily accepted the fruit. The new girl quickly ate every last morsel of the orange, then licked her fingers. Shyly, she smiled at Jae-Mi. Jae-Mi had never seen the skinny, serious-looking girl smile before.

"You're welcome," Jae-Mi said in English.

"Wel-come," Kyoko repeated.

Jae-Mi shook her head. "No, you're supposed to say, 'Thank you' first."

"Thank-you-first," Kyoko said.

Jae-Mi laughed. Confused, Kyoko smiled again. Although each could speak very little that the other understood, Jae-Mi and Kyoko began eating lunch together every day. Jae-Mi shared her orange and

Kyoko shared her rice ball. Kyoko bravely tasted spicy *kimchee* and Jae-Mi was surprised to discover that Kyoko's mother's pickles were quite tasty.

One afternoon after school, Jae-Mi decided to show Kyoko how to play the Korean seesaw jumping game. They went to the dump and found a board, which they balanced on an old bag of sand left over from the dining room construction. Each girl stood on one end and they took turns jumping.

"Hold still," Jae-Mi said. "Keep your balance."

Kyoko looked at her curiously. She watched as Jae-Mi made a little jump on her end. The force of her landing propelled Kyoko up into the air a few inches. She squealed with surprise. When she landed on the board again, her jump sent Jae-Mi flying. Back and forth they practiced jumping. Sometimes one of them would tumble into the dirt. Sometimes they would land with both feet and cheer.

"Let me try!" Hi-Jong insisted when she saw Jae-Mi and the new girl from school.

"Just a minute," Jae-Mi said. "We are trying for a perfect bounce."

The girls' laughter soon brought a crowd of some of the other Korean children from nearby. "Who's she?" demanded Minja, the big girl the sisters had met on their first day in Riverside.

"She's new," Jae-Mi replied.

"Doesn't she talk?"

Nervously, Jae-Mi jumped again. "She doesn't know much English."

"Does she know Korean?"

"A few words." Jae-Mi gulped and tried to change the subject. "Do you want to try, Minja?"

"It's my turn," Hi-Jong insisted, her lower lip sticking out in a pout. "Tell the Jap to play on her own seesaw."

Jae-Mi shot her sister a threatening look.

"Jap?" Minja asked in a menacing voice.

Kyoko paused, still as a cat on the end of the board. Her eyes darted toward Jae-Mi. She sniffed as if sensing danger. Carefully, she stepped from the board and began to back away. "Garlic eater," she whispered in English.

Minja curled her fists and took a few steps forward. She was nearly twice Kyoko's size. Clearly she'd be finished with this invader in no time.

"Leave her alone," Jae-Mi said quietly. "She's my friend."

"She's a Jap." Minja picked up the seesaw board in her big, beefy hands. "She shouldn't be here, doesn't she know?"

Hi-Jong gulped. Her eyes darted from the board to her sister, from the board to the Japanese girl. What had she done?

"Leave her alone," Jae-Mi repeated.

But Minja didn't seem to hear her. She began waving the board in the air high over her head. Kyoko ducked and stumbled backward. "Think you can call me a garlic-eater, do you?"

Jae-Mi tried to remember what Father had told them. She tried to remember the part about ignorance and violence, but she knew Minja wouldn't listen. The Korean girl kept waving the board as if she were enjoying watching Kyoko cower and plead in her incomprehensible language.

Minja hooted. "Can't understand a word, Jap."

Kyoko edged backward toward the railroad track. She had only to cross the track and run back to the Japanese part of town and then she'd be safe. But Kyoko was so skinny, so frail that she kept falling. All Jae-Mi could think of was the neck-choppers on the playground. They had probably really bruised some-one as little as Kyoko. *Why didn't I do anything?*

Minja plunged forward and waved the board as easily as if she were batting away flies. Her distorted face was filled with pleasure. And something else. Something Jae-Mi remembered from that terrible day in San Francisco. The howling, mad rush of those men on the dock. Their lips had curled like those of wild dogs, the same way Minja's mouth looked at this very moment.

"Stop!" Jae-Mi shouted.

Minja paid no attention. She meant to hurt Kyoko.

Hurt her badly. Kyoko scrambled over the rails onto the tracks and stood frozen, one foot twisted and caught under the rail.

"Hey!" Minja shouted. "Hey, Jap! Come over here." She waved the board high in the air. Just as she was about to bring it down on Kyoko's head, something snapped in Jae-Mi. She saw white. Nothing but white as she threw herself against the bigger girl. Jae-Mi hit Minja hard and knocked the board from her hand.

Minja gave Jae-Mi a swift punch, leaned over, and scooped up the board. She brandished it like a weapon, like a sword, and smacked Jae-Mi against the shoulder. Jae-Mi reeled. She tripped over the heaps of gravel along the railroad bed. Small sharp stones dug into her palms and her knees. She didn't notice. As fast as she could, she was on her feet.

She charged Minja again. Minja raised the board in the air. She teetered along the rail, ready to make one last well-placed swat, when suddenly the ground began to shake and tremble.

Hi-Jong screamed and pointed, but Jae-Mi couldn't hear her sister's warning. She was too full of blind rage. Only when she looked at Minja's pale face did she understand.

Train!

Minja leapt. Jae-Mi dove and tumbled off the track just as the train roared past. Grit flew. A horn blared.

A great rush of wind and steel and deadly wheels sucked away all available oxygen as the train howled and thundered past.

"Kyoko!" Jae-Mi screamed.

Stunned, Jae-Mi and Hi-Jong stood watching helplessly, freight car after freight car. The dizzying parade of wheels and steel. Jae-Mi could not move. She could not think. She did not even notice Minja, mouth trembling, drop the board and run away.

Finally, after what seemed forever, the last car careened past. Jae-Mi barely dared to look. But when she did, she was amazed to see Kyoko standing on the other side of the track, bent over, gasping for air.

After a moment, Kyoko raised her gaze and stared at Jae-Mi with betrayed, hopeless eyes—like a ghost, like a tortured spirit. Then she dashed away, back to the place where she came from on the other side of the tracks.

Jae-Mi turned to her sister, but did not say anything. They had both almost witnessed a death because of one cruel word. They couldn't say that word. They couldn't think that word. They would tell no one of what happened here. Not even Su-Na. It was their awful secret.

Shaken and silent, they went home. Hi-Jong went to gather wood. Jae-Mi had lunch pails to clean. The men were laughing and joking, but Jae-Mi didn't notice. All she could see was the rush of dirt and wind.

Her ears were still filled with the deafening sound of grinding steel wheels. Wearily, she picked up the returned lunch buckets. They seemed heavier than they should be. She opened one, then another, then another. A group of Mother's customers began to laugh at their practical joke.

"No more oranges, sorry," one of the smiling men said. "But we were afraid you'd scold us if we didn't bring you something."

Bewildered, Jae-Mi dumped the buckets on the ground. Rocks tumbled out one by one.

"Good joke, huh?"

None of the men could understand why Jae-Mi was crying.

Chapter

10

The name you call me
is not my real name.
Even a swallow knows his neighbor's call.
I wish I could tell someone
how sad I am.

Summer disappeared too quickly. Another dreadful school year began. When winter returned once more, Su-Na complained to her father that she needed a new coat to wear to school. Her old jacket was too small. She was secretly hoping that this might serve as an excuse not to go to school. She had begun to notice that their walk through town took them past more and more people who seemed to curse and stare at them. At almost every corner men stood about in slouch hats and dirty clothes waiting beside boarded-up businesses. Su-Na did not know what they were waiting for. The stores were not going to open again. When she asked who the men were, Mother said they were out of work.

Su-Na was surprised when she came home one afternoon and discovered that Father had sewn her and her sisters beautiful new coats. "He worked late at night for three nights to make you these," Mother said proudly. Since they did not have a sewing machine, he had sewed each coat by hand. They were made out of identical red material and were exactly the same design except that each was slightly larger than the next.

Jai-Mi and Hi-Jong gasped when they saw the coats. "Beautiful!" Jae-Mi said.

"The most beautiful thing I have ever seen," Hi-Jong said. Neither she nor her middle sister knew that Father was so clever.

"Tailoring was how he made his living in Korea," Mother explained. She picked up Edward in her arms and placed him in his bed. "What's wrong with you, Su-Na? Don't you like the coat?"

Su-Na nodded. She tried very hard to smile. Yet she knew that the next morning she would have to wear the same bright coat as all her sisters. They would have to walk together to school. What would the other children say? She did not want to look like her sisters, who were younger and two grades below her. Su-Na was nearly fourteen and she wanted to look grown-up. At the same time she didn't want to insult her father and all his hard work.

The next morning, Su-Na hurried out the door without the coat, planning to say she had forgotten it.

"Come back!" called Hi-Jong. "You have forgotten your wonderful red jacket." She ran breathlessly to her sister and gave Su-Na the coat. The three sisters walked together the rest of the way to school.

Just as Su-Na had feared, she was no longer invisible. Everyone on the street in Riverside noticed her and her sisters.

"Business must be very good down by the tracks," a man grumbled.

"Too good," said another.

"Taking jobs from decent Americans."

The way the men looked at her and her sisters made Su-Na nervous. She would have to remember to walk a different way tomorrow. "Hurry," she told her sisters.

When they arrived on the playground, the children in tattered overalls stopped playing and jeered. Instead of feeling special, Su-Na felt as if everyone were making fun of her.

"I don't care," Jai-Mi said. "Let them say what they want."

"They're just jealous," Hi-Jong agreed. She smoothed the lovely folds of the material that Father had bought in town. Each coat had shiny black buttons and one pocket. The collars turned up so that when the wind blew, their necks would stay warm. To Hi-Jong, the red coat was perfect.

Su-Na quickly parted from her sisters. She hurried into the outhouse, removed the coat, and rolled it into a tight ball. The bell rang. Now she knew she was going to be in trouble, but she didn't care. When she was certain no one was looking, she stuffed the coat under a nearby bush. As soon as school ended, she'd come outside, find it, and take it home. No one would see her wearing it.

When school ended that day, Su-Na rushed outside. She felt strangely happy. For the first time her teacher had pinned one of her poems on the bulletin board. Seeing it there with her name in neat blue pen made her feel very special. All the way home she recited the little poem so that she could tell her mother:

Pine tree on the mountain
leans against a rock.
Are you sleeping or only resting?
Snow will come soon
and cover you with a blanket.

Halfway home Su-Na remembered the red coat. Panic-stricken, she turned and dashed back through town, taking the short cut down Main Street to save time. She gritted her teeth and ran as fast as she could past the lingering men who had no jobs.

"Where you going in such a hurry?" one said.

" 'Ladybug, ladybug fly away home.' "

She knew enough to run through the street, not on the sidewalk. If she walked on the sidewalk, someone was always trying to block her way with an outstretched foot. She ran faster, filled with panic now. The sun was beginning to set. What if she could not find the coat in the darkness?

Su-Na searched desperately around the outhouse. She looked under every bush, every tree. But there was no coat. Perhaps someone had found it and taken it into school. Her face was streaming with sweat. What would Father and Mother say when she came home without the coat? How would she explain where it was?

Terror-stricken, she began the long walk home. This time she walked through the outskirts of town along the railroad track so that she could avoid Main Street. Deep in thought, she tried to come up with an excuse. What would she say? Could she sound convincing?

Suddenly she looked up and saw a strange orange glow in the distance. At first she thought it was the light from a train. Perhaps an accident? But as she looked more carefully she realized that smoke was curling high overhead. The air was thick with the acrid smell of burning wood.

Su-Na broke into a run. She gulped for air, pushing her legs as fast as they could carry her. She felt as if she were in a nightmare. No matter how hard she tried, she could not make her legs move faster. "Mother! Father!" she screamed as the burning dining hall came into view.

Someone grabbed her and held her tight so that she would not run any closer. It was Mrs. Paik. "They're all right. Your sisters and brothers are safe, too, thank God."

Su-Na took a great breath of relief.

Quickly, the walls of the flimsy dining hall crumpled like paper. The roof flattened and caved in. Two more houses burst into flame from the flying hot cinders. Up and down the track people rushed around with buckets of water from the pumps to stop the leapfrogging, but it was too little, too late. Sparks and cinders flew up into the sky.

Everything Su-Na's family owned, everything they hoped for was vanishing in flame. She began to shake uncontrollably. "Why? Why did this happen?"

"No one knows for sure. A simple accident maybe," Mrs. Paik said slowly. She stroked Su-Na's hair. "Or something else. Things not good. Not now. Too much hatred. Jealousy." Gently, Mrs. Paik cupped Su-Na's face with her hands and looked at her carefully, closely. "Your father and mother are stubborn. You convince them. Move. Go somewhere else. Get out of here while you can."

Somewhere else? Su-Na trembled with fear. Everything was gone. Everything they owned. *We can never go back to Korea.*

The next two weeks unrolled like a scroll painted with a nightmare. Su-Na and her sisters did not go to school. And yet they did not play or amuse themselves. The business was gone and so was their only source of income. The family struggled to find enough to eat and keep from starving to death. When the dining hall caught fire, their nearby house also went up in flames. Mother and the children had escaped just in time. Father, who had been away in the orchards, had run all the way home when he saw the smoke.

Nothing was left. Even the precious photograph that had come with them from Korea had burned. Their money, their bedding, what little extra clothing they had was gone. All the equipment, dishes, and food they had borrowed from the Chinese store owner was destroyed. Not only were they penniless, they now owed money. Father stood in the rubble and pushed the cinders with his boot toe and could not find even one chopstick left worth saving.

So many other people in the Korean and Chinese section of town had lost their homes, their businesses, that there was much want, much hunger. Su-Na's family went to live with Mr. and Mrs. Paik in their one-room house but it was very crowded. The babies cried and no one could sleep. Days passed. Su-Na and her sisters wished that they could go back to school, a place that might not be so crowded, so dirty, so hopeless. But Mother said no. It was too dangerous now.

Mother managed to convince the one store owner left in town to sell her a small bag of flour. She added some water and cooked some tiny biscuits in Mrs. Paik's oven. Su-Na, her sisters, and Mrs. Paik's three children each received one little biscuit and a cup of water for their meals for two days. Su-Na's stomach growled. Her brothers cried for more food.

When Su-Na and her sisters went to the slaughterhouse, there was nothing left. Not one scrap. Every last bit of refuse had been cleaned up by children from other hungry families. Even the dump was picked clean. The next Saturday that Su-Na and her sisters went to collect, they left even earlier. This time when they arrived they discovered that the slaughterhouse had a sign nailed over the door. "Closed for business."

Su-Na could hardly believe she once dreaded this place, hated this place. Now she wished more than anything that it was still open. She'd scramble on the ground if she had to, her stomach felt that empty. She could see the hunger on her sisters' faces, too. But most pathetic of all was the way the baby cried and cried.

"How will we live?" Jae-Mi asked her sisters. She was tired of gnawing hunger, only made worse by eating something as small as a biscuit. She was tired of feeling dirty and homeless.

"Father will think of something. He always does," Su-Na said, even though she did not feel very hopeful.

There was no work in the citrus groves because there was no one to buy the fruit. Oranges and lemons rotted in piles. Everywhere outside of Riverside, Father said, businesses were going bankrupt. America was not the land of plenty they had once believed. Worse yet, when Father went to the police station to insist that someone investigate the fires that had been started by an arsonist, he was thrown in jail.

This terrified Mother. She spoke little English and all she could think about was what happened to people who went to jail in Korea. They never came out.

"Where do you think you're going?" Mrs. Paik demanded when she saw Mother gathering up the baby and Meung and her daughters.

"To get my husband back," Mother said. She marched into the downtown where Su-Na and her sisters had been forbidden to go. Nervous, Su-Na carried the baby. Mother took Meung by the hand. Jae-Mi and Hi-Jong trailed behind. "What happens if they put us in jail, too?" Hi-Jong demanded.

Su-Na shot a threatening glance at her sister. "Be quiet."

When they finally arrived at the police station, Su-Na had to speak English for her mother. The building had a sour smell and it was filled with white faces and large men in dark uniforms. Mother marched to the desk with all her children trailing behind her. She shoved Su-Na forward and told her exactly what to say.

"Honorable sir, we look for our father," Su-Na said. Her face felt hot with embarrassment. She could tell that the large man behind the desk was amused. He smiled down at her. She sniffed. On his desk was a round sweet bread. Su-Na kept looking at the food and wishing she could taste it. She had trouble concentrating. Mother whispered frantically in her ear, "Please tell us where he is and when he will be released. His family is in great want."

"Your father will be here overnight for disturbing the peace," the man said.

"Disturbing the peace? What does that mean?" Su-Na asked. Her mother yanked again on her arm as if she could tell this was something ominous.

"He came in here screaming and yelling and making all sorts of wild accusations about proper citizens of Riverside," the officer said. "That's why he got locked up."

"Locked up?" Su-Na asked. She did not understand these terrible words. Had Father been hurt? Was he dead?

"Locked up means put in jail. Now, I've got some

important business to attend to. Can you get your mother and the rest of this brood out of here?" A few other policemen in the room began to chuckle. "They're beginning to stink up the place."

Su-Na's eyes narrowed. She could see that this man was not going to help them. She had seen it all before in the principal's office and on the playground and in the slaughterhouse doorway. This man did not consider her or her family human beings. She clenched her fists. "This America is a free country, is it not?" Su-Na asked. She had learned this in school. This was what the thick blue book said. She had read it with her own eyes. "Everyone is equal."

"Free country for citizens," the officer said, imitating her accent in a way that only made her more furious. "But your father is not a citizen. He can't vote. He can't own land. He has no rights. Now get out of here. If we see fit, he'll be released tomorrow. *Understand-ee?*"

Su-Na swallowed hard. "How do I know what you say is true?" she demanded. "Can we see him and make sure he is all right?"

The man looked down at them and shook his head. "Too many of you, sorry. Eight A.M. tomorrow he'll be released. Come back then. That's the best I can do. Now be on your way. Better yet, go back to Japan or China or wherever you came from. That would suit me just fine."

"Sir, you are very ignorant man," Su-Na said, eyes narrowing. "We are not from China or Japan. We are from Korea."

"Get!" the officer replied, his face red. "Before I change my mind." He pointed a stubby finger toward the door.

Mother kept whispering over and over in Su-Na's ear in an insistent, irritating manner, "What does he say? What does he say?"

Disgusted and overwhelmed by a feeling of helplessness, Su-Na took her sisters' and brothers' hands and began herding her family out the door. "Come! Come on! Let's get out of here."

When they were finally outside again where they could breathe, Su-Na told her mother that Father would be released the next day. Mother seemed overjoyed. She embraced Su-Na as if she herself had somehow convinced the police officer to let Father go.

"Mother," Su-Na said, focusing all her attention on her mother's hopeful eyes, "we must get out of here. We must leave this place however we can. You must find a way. Borrow the money—anything. Do you understand?"

Mother nodded. She began walking with determination down the sidewalk with the baby in her arms. Su-Na and the other children followed.

Father was released the next day. And somehow Mother scraped the money together for third-class train tickets for everyone in the family. They would head north, Father said wearily. He had heard from the son of an old neighbor from Seoul about jobs in a mining town. That afternoon they packed their few meager borrowed belongings, a comb, a blanket, a bottle of water, and a bit of food wrapped up in a cloth, and said a tearful good-bye to the Paik family.

"We start over again," Father promised in a bright voice. They stood on the train platform waiting for the train. Su-Na and her sisters looked down the long, endless track and said nothing. Edward whimpered softly.

"About the red coat, Father," Su-Na began. "I want to explain what happened—"

"Do not speak of it," Father said. He peered down the empty track. The muscle in his jaw quivered.

"But I want to tell you—"

Father turned to her and glared. His face was flushed. "You never listen, do you? Always headstrong, always careless, always criticizing. Speaking when you should not. Silence!"

His hand flashed out and something hot suddenly burned against Su-Na's cheek. She stumbled backward in shock. Blinking hard, she cupped her hand against her stinging face.

"Su-Na?" Mother murmured and stepped toward her as if to give her daughter comfort.

"You, woman! Be silent for once! When a hen crows like a rooster, it brings ruin to a home." Father glowered hatefully at Mother. He raised his fist, but Mother did not budge. She did not say one word. Slowly, Father lowered his arm. He tucked his trembling hand in his pocket and stomped to the other end of the platform where he stood alone.

Jae-Mi and Hi-Jong were too shocked to speak. No one moved. No one breathed.

"Where going?" Meung asked, suddenly breaking the silence. He pulled insistently on Su-Na's skirt. "Hungry."

"Hush," Su-Na said. *I will not let him see me cry. No.* In the distance she could hear the lonesome whistle of the train. The wail sounded almost as forlorn and hopeless as she felt.

Chapter

11

Idria, California

1908

In this faraway place the snow has melted,
Dark clouds hover overhead.
Where are the early blossoms
That should be blooming now?
Standing alone in the sunset,
I think I have lost my way.

"Beyond mountains are mountains," Mother liked to say whenever anyone felt discouraged. Su-Na and her sisters never understood that old saying until they began their journey to Idria, a small mining town in the mountains nearly three hundred miles to the north.

There always seemed to be another mountain, another hill that the slow train struggled to climb. The children soon grew impatient that they would ever arrive.

After the train ride finally ended, they journeyed in a big hay wagon with benches on both sides. Four horses pulled the wagon up the mountains. The rancher driving the wagon had just delivered a load of hay and was on his way back to Idria. He kindly agreed to give Su-Na's family a ride. "Hop in," he said. He was a large man in overalls and a large sweat-stained hat. He spoke very little most of the way but seemed grateful for the company.

Once they headed into the mountains, the air changed. Jae-Mi sniffed. The cool, refreshing breeze of early spring made her shiver. When she breathed the thin mountain air through her nose, she felt dizzy and inexplicably happy. She felt glad to have escaped from hot, dry Riverside where the wind was always blowing and the air felt gritty and the grown-ups were always angry or worried. Even her parents' faces seemed to have changed. Their expressions were softer, as if they were thinking about something very far away.

"A new kind of world," Hi-Jong murmured as the wagon bounced along. She looked out at the pine trees and the rocks and the distant mountain ranges dusted with snow. The blue sky was filled with white shiplike clouds outlined in sharp relief. There was a sense of freedom here, of space, of pine-scented air.

"The best place so far," agreed Jae-Mi, who sat beside her. Sometimes they crossed clear, rushing streams. Other times the wagon tipped precariously as they rounded another bend up a pine-covered hill. Several times Father had to climb out of the wagon and help move rocks that had rolled onto the narrow, rutted, muddy road. Whenever this happened, Father avoided looking at Su-Na. He did not speak to her or apologize for what had happened on the train platform in Riverside. He never spoke of it again.

Su-Na sat in front with the rancher and said very little on the journey. Once again she slipped skillfully into invisibility. She felt grateful to have escaped from Riverside. But she also sensed that something had changed irrevocably between herself and Father. She couldn't name it. She only knew that sadness lingered and tasted bitter in her mouth.

"What's that?" Jae-Mi asked in English. She pointed up into the mountainside. There was a large yellowish scar slashed on the side of the hill with a gaping hole and a large forbidding fence crisscrossed with barbed wire. Around the hole were no trees, no sign of life.

"Quicksilver mine," the rancher said. "Only a few in the United States. Largest one's here in Idria. Beyond the mine's the furnaces where they process the stuff. Won't see anything alive there. The fumes kill faster than strychnine poison."

"What's quicksilver?" asked Su-Na, who translated everything into Korean over her shoulder so that Mother and Father could understand.

The rancher scratched the back of his neck. "All I know is they make explosives with it. I expect that's why they got soldiers guarding the mines."

Father leaned forward and hissed in Su-Na's ear. "My father," Su-Na continued, "would like to know if there are any jobs in the mine."

The rancher shrugged. "Could be. I heard in town last week they's looking for some replacements in the furnace. That's a nasty place." He turned and looked at Father, who was perhaps only half his size. "Pay's five dollars a day. Awful lot of money, sure, but nobody lasts long in there."

"Five dollars!" Father exclaimed when Su-Na told him. He seemed overjoyed. "Think how quickly I can repay my debts if I make that much money!"

Su-Na nodded and tried not to appear discouraging. *What if they don't hire Koreans?* She stared over her shoulder at the ominous scar in the side of the hill.

"Where you folks from?" the rancher asked.

"Riverside," Su-Na said carefully. She watched him out of the corner of her eye for any sudden coldness, any whiff of superiority. She saw none.

"And before that, where you from?"

"Hawaii." *Careful now. Here it comes.*

"And before that?"

"Korea." Su-Na studied him closely.

He scratched the back of his neck and looked puzzled. "Can't say I ever heard of Korea. I'm from Kansas City myself."

Su-Na relaxed and leaned back in the seat. "Korea's between Japan and China on the other side of the world. Far, far away."

"Too far to go back?"

Su-Na crossed her arms in front of herself. "I don't think I'll ever go back," she said, surprised to hear the words spoken aloud. She had never told anyone before. Not even her sisters.

"Can't say I blame you. Got to put down roots someplace. Here's as good as any. That's what I always tell my wife. She's from Indiana. She don't want to go back where she came from either."

Here's as good as any. Su-Na smiled.

"Are there tigers here?" Mother asked nervously. She scanned the distant hills.

Father laughed. "No tigers. Those were in Korea long, long ago." It was good to hear Father laugh again. He, too, seemed reinvigorated.

"Will we ever arrive?" Hi-Jong asked impatiently. She was hungry and tired and dusty. Meung, now nearly three, scrambled about the wagon, begging for food. Mother unwrapped a small piece of precious cheese from a handkerchief, broke away a tiny section, and carefully popped it into his mouth.

When he demanded more, she gave him another chunk.

"There won't be any for the rest of us," Hi-Jong complained. She was holding in her lap Edward, an unusually large one-year-old who looked about placidly and sucked his chubby thumb.

"Your eldest brother is hungry," replied Mother, who always fed her sons the choicest bits of whatever small meal they might have. It was, she said, the custom. But Hi-Jong was certain it was because Mother loved Meung and Edward best.

Finally they reached the little mountain town of Idria, tucked away on a high dry ridge of spiny mountains and scrubby hills. They thanked the rancher, who pointed out the mining office. Quickly, they scrambled off the wagon. Father wasted no time in hurrying in to apply for a job, using Su-Na as his translator. Su-Na secretly felt embarrassed having to tell her father the words the white mine manager said. But after her experience in the police station in Riverside, she realized the power of understanding English. She only wished one day her parents would learn how to speak well enough that they would not have to depend as much on her or her brothers or sisters.

"Did you get the job?" Mother asked eagerly when Su-Na and Father returned to them on the street after signing some papers.

Father nodded happily. Su-Na smiled. She was delighted that no one refused them because they were Korean. No one seemed to care. She was also aware, however, that the job was considered difficult and dangerous. Father's only protection, the manager had said, would be a piece of cloth tied over his nose and mouth. When the mine manager asked three times if Father understood what he was getting into, Father acted even more eager. "Yes, yes, yes," he kept repeating in English. "Please, please, please."

Father's obvious desperation made Su-Na even more humiliated. Of course, she tried not to let this show. Father would lose face if he knew how his begging bothered her.

To Mother's delight, they found an old house to rent. It had four small rooms and a shack in back to serve as the kitchen with two large tubs. This was the place where Mother decided she would set up a laundry business. The house had no electricity. There was a small wood stove to provide heat and a cooking fire. The water pump stood outside the house and the outhouse was down the hill.

After living for months in the cramped one-room quarters with the Paik family, the house seemed enormous and wonderful to Su-Na and her sisters. Father was given credit at the company store to buy a kerosene lamp, a bag of rice, and something amazing—a big ham. Su-Na and her sisters had never eaten such a luxury. Before they prepared their first meal, Father decided to take everyone into the hills to go hunting. He took a basket and an old feed sack and motioned for Su-Na, Hi-Jong, and Jae-Mi to follow him. Little Meung came along, too. Mother and Edward stayed behind and rested.

Hungrily, the children followed, not really knowing what was going to happen. Ahead they heard the sound of rushing water. "Over here!" Father called to them. Su-Na took Meung by the hand and ran around the trees and rocks. It seemed like a game. She could not remember when she had seen Father seem so happy and youthful. He was acting like a young boy. "Look!" he cried.

In the shallow water where the current was still, strange creatures scurried in and out of shadows. They looked like insects with long pincer claws on each of their front arms. "Crayfish. Very good to eat," Father said. He crouched at the water's edge, carefully leaned over the water so that the scuttling creatures could not sense his shadow. Slowly, he rolled up his sleeve and lowered his hand in the water.

Su-Na and her sisters held their breath. Suddenly, his hand reemerged with a wriggling, furious crayfish. Hi-Jong stifled a scream. "Let me try!" Jae-Mi insisted. Beside a rock she spied something creeping. She leaned forward on her hands and knees and slowly lowered her hand into the icy cold water. As soon as she touched the slimy, wiggling crayfish, she wanted to drop it. But she didn't. She clutched him tightly and pulled him dripping and flailing out of the water. Her sisters cheered.

They caught a dozen more crayfish and put them in the sack and walked on. Farther upstream, Father pointed out a lovely green floating plant in a shallow place near a spring. He gathered this up and showed the girls how to pick the sweet, new watercress. He nibbled a little bit of the fresh green leaf. "Very tasty," he said.

The girls laughed. "What about this?" Hi-Jong said. She pointed to a plant with pointy leaves, purple flowers, and bright red berries.

"Never, never eat that. It's poison," Father said in a serious voice. "Pick and eat only what I show you. Just as there are good and bad people in the world, there are good and bad plants for eating. Knowing which is which will save you a lot of trouble and stomachaches."

Jae-Mi and her sisters learned how to find the first wild celery with thin and tender leaves. He showed them which bushes would grow gooseberries and blackberries later in the summer and where they would be sure to find wild raspberries. "How do you know so much?" Jae-Mi asked Father as they started back with their basket full of greens and the sack full of crayfish.

"I learned as a boy in the hills and streams where I

grew up," he said with a catch in his voice. "Someday I'll take you to those hills when we go home."

"Home," Jae-Mi said half-aloud. She pondered this word. To Father she knew that home meant Korea. She did not want to tell him that she could barely remember the place they had left behind nearly four years earlier. She did not think of Korea as her home anymore. Her home was here in America. But Father was in such an unusually good mood, she did not want to spoil it by bringing up unpleasant ideas and destroying the good *ki-bun*.

That evening Mother made a splendid feast of the rice, ham, crayfish, and delicious vegetables. Father said a special grace thanking God for leading them to this place. Su-Na and her sisters and brothers ate and ate. For once they were full and satisfied.

That night when she went outside to dump the dish water, Mother called to her family. "Come out and see," she said. Su-Na and her sisters joined her and looked up at the enormous sky scattered with stars. When they lived in Riverside, the sky was never this clear, this bright. In the high altitude the stars glittered brilliantly. They seemed enormous and nearly pressing against their faces as they looked up in wonder.

"So many," Hi-Jong whispered.

"More than I can count," Jae-Mi said.

Meung giggled and reached out his hand as if he

might touch the stars. Su-Na alone looked up and said nothing. She was too busy making a wish.

The next day Father went to work. Su-Na and her sisters helped Mother set up her laundry business. They gathered firewood and found an extra old tub and strung lines among the trees. Then they went from house to house asking if people had any clothes that needed washing. Su-Na was pleased that no one slammed a door in their faces and a few bachelors seemed happy to have someone do their wash. The girls carried the big bundles of clothing back to the house.

"Now I have another chore for you," Mother said as soon as Edward fell asleep on his little mat and Meung was busy building a house with sticks and rocks in the dirt beside the back step. "I want you to go over the hill and find out about the school. Tomorrow you must start your studies again."

Jae-Mi howled with disappointment. "Everything is so perfect! Why do we have to spoil it with school?"

Mother frowned. "School is important. Su-Na, take the girls and sign them up."

Su-Na sighed. Although she missed reading books and writing on plentiful paper, she did not want to go to school again. All that she remembered were the neck-choppers and the loneliness. But she knew that she had to obey. "Come on," she grumbled, as they began their journey that afternoon. "Maybe it won't be so bad."

The schoolhouse here was nothing like the dark, brick building in Riverside. It was a simple, unpainted, one-story frame building with a tin chimney sticking out of the top of a shingled roof. The schoolhouse had four windows. Nearby stood two outhouses. A cluster of pine trees leaned at one end of a grassy open area. There were no swings, no playground. Just an open field.

"That's it?" Jae-Mi asked in amazement.

Hi-Jong sucked in her lips and made a backward whistle. "How does it fit everybody?"

Su-Na shrugged. "Let's go see." They walked slowly toward the schoolhouse and could hear many voices. Some were talking. Some were laughing. Some were shouting. They peeked in the doorway. The one room had desks on each side crowded with thirty children of all ages. In the middle of the room was a wood-burning stove. As soon as she and her sisters stepped near the doorway, someone said something and suddenly everyone turned and looked in their direction.

"Hello," Su-Na said bravely, expecting the worst.

"*Buenos dias,*" the children hooted back their greeting. A little wad of paper darted through the air and landed at Hi-Jong's feet. She picked it up and smoothed it out. The paper had a funny face drawn on it. The hair was sticking out and the eyes were crossed.

When Su-Na surveyed the classroom, she couldn't find the teacher. Where was she? As she looked around, Su-Na spied very few white children. Unlike the students at the grade school in Riverside, almost everyone was speaking Spanish. No one sang "Ching Chong China Man." No one tried to chop her or her sisters in the neck.

"Come in!" an older girl said in English. She had long dark hair and was wearing a bright yellow dress. "Miss Teacher will be right back."

Su-Na grabbed her sisters and took a few steps into the room. No one tripped her. No one jeered at her or called her names. Her shoulders straightened. She spied an empty table and part of a bench that was empty. She and her sisters slid onto the bench. Hi-Jong, still terrified, kept her hands clasped tightly together.

Su-Na studied the blackboard. Someone had written a poem in English about a lovely tree. Su-Na smiled. She could read the poem, every word. Jae-Mi didn't pay any attention to the blackboard. She kept her eye on the boys who were throwing small wads of paper. She turned to Su-Na and said happily, "I like this place."

Chapter

12

In the mountains my true freedom dwells.
I am myself, not the worthless girl
ancestors praised.
If you see me among fragrant pines,
smile and greet me.

When the teacher returned, Su-Na noticed right away that the woman had very large ears and eyes the color of Grandmother's prized pale green porcelain bowl. Neither she nor her sisters had ever seen anyone with eyes that color. Her wavy hair was the color of varnished wood. Her lips were thin and she wore a black shirtwaist dress with a black skirt. The edges of her worn sleeves were frayed and white.

There was so much noise and commotion in the room the teacher didn't notice Su-Na and her sisters at first. The students passed the only book in the room down row upon row to practice reading. The children kicked their heels, drummed their desks, and joked while they waited their turns. The room was very noisy. Before the book reached Su-Na and her sisters, the morning ended. The teacher rang a bell and everyone thundered out to the field for afternoon recess. Only then did the teacher notice the three newcomers in the back of the room.

"Hello," she said in a hoarse voice. Wearily, she sat down on her chair behind the table with the bunch of wildflowers in a preserves jar of water. "What are your names?"

Su-Na started making a little self-conscious bow until she caught herself. As usual, she did all the talking. She explained where they had come from but did not give the embarrassing details about their house and business burning down or the part about their father being held in the police station overnight.

"You speak very good English," the woman said. Her name was Miss Van Shauk, which was nearly impossible to remember so everyone called her Miss V. "How old are you?"

"Fourteen," Su-Na replied. "I can read and write English."

"Very good. You're almost old enough for high school. And you?"

Hi-Jong and Jae-Mi shyly introduced themselves.

"I'm eleven," Jae-Mi said. "And she's ten. What's high school?"

Miss V fluttered her hand slightly. "Where a student goes after he or she has mastered the work at this level. There are more books, more subjects—literature, poetry, history, science. Not everyone goes, of course. You have to pass a difficult test first to show you're ready."

Su-Na's ears pricked up. *Poetry.* She wanted to know more about high school. "How much does it cost?"

"I'm not sure exactly. The nearest high school is in Willows. You have to buy your own books and supplies and find your own place to live."

Su-Na's shoulders sagged. High school sounded expensive.

"Of course, you may be able to board with a family and help around the house. That's what I did to help pay my way." Miss V smiled. She had very even teeth.

Su-Na knew her family had no extra money and was deep in debt. High school would be considered an extravagance. And yet, if it were only possible! She looked around the classroom. "Do you suppose you might have a job for me? I can clean. I can sweep. I know how to chop wood." She kept talking, faster now. "I can wipe off the blackboard and ring the bell so the children know it's time to come in." Her face flushed. She knew her sisters would make fun of her later for sounding so eager, so idiotic.

Miss V smiled. "Perhaps I can ask the school supervisor if there's any money in the budget. We'll see."

Su-Na thanked her teacher, bowing, and hurried home with her sisters. They knew Mother would be waiting for them to help with the laundry. Su-Na was so excited about what Miss V had said, she hardly heard her sisters speaking. Wouldn't Father be pleased? He said he always wanted a scholar in the family. As for Mother, she might take some convincing—

"You really want to go to high school?" Jae-Mi demanded. She glanced at Su-Na in disgust as they climbed up the hill toward their house.

"She might get a new dress to wear," Hi-Jong said. "If I could have a new dress and a new pair of shoes, I would want to go to high school, too."

Little by little, the days grew longer. School was such a pleasure, Su-Na felt sad when the term ended. Summer came. Father worked long hours in the furnace area and came home even more exhausted than he had from the orange groves. "I am becoming an old man," he said with a weary half-grin. He lay down upon the bed and stayed there until dinner.

When fall returned again, Su-Na was delighted to begin school. There never seemed a good time for Su-Na to bring up the subject of high school with Father. In spite of this fact, she worked very hard to catch up with the schoolwork she had missed. Miss V seemed delighted to have a serious student at last and worked on mathematics with Su-Na early in the morning before school and after school when Su-Na finished cleaning the classroom.

One early October morning while standing among the flapping pieces of laundry, Jae-Mi and Hi-Jong asked Mother if the next day they could go into the mountains to search for wild berries. "Only if you go with Su-Na," she said. She pinned up three more towels quickly.

They had to wait until after Su-Na was finished cleaning the classroom for Miss V. Su-Na felt fortunate to receive one quarter every day she did the work. Her sisters sat impatiently outside on the step. An older Mexican boy who wasn't in their class came out the door. They couldn't see his face very well. He tipped his hat to them and kept walking.

"Who was that?" Jae-Mi asked when Su-Na finally appeared, her cleaning finished.

"Oh," Su-Na said quickly. "Just someone who delivers firewood each week."

"Your face is flushed," Hi-Jong said. She swung the berry basket on her arm.

"I've been sweeping while you have been sitting," Su-Na shot back in a loud voice.

"Careful now, not so noisy! You'll invite bad spirits," Jae-Mi said, delighted to have made her sister so furious. "Isn't that the stupid old Korean rule? If you're a woman, be seen and not heard?"

Su-Na stomped ahead. "Come back!" Hi-Jong called. "We were only joking. We cannot go into the mountains unless you come with us. Mother said."

Su-Na grumbled something her sisters couldn't hear. They walked quickly up the path into the cool, pine-scented air. The wind felt good on Su-Na's flushed face. Life had become very confusing. Sometimes she felt very happy. A second later she became furious with the whole world. Some days she cried and cried for absolutely no reason. Her moods, Mother said, were as changeable and unpredictable as the weather.

"Be friends again," Jae-Mi said in a coaxing voice. She took Su-Na by the hand and for several moments no one spoke. Because night came more quickly now, they did not have much time to hunt for berries. They scrambled along a familiar rocky ledge that they had visited many times since their arrival in Idria.

"Here!" Hi-Jong announced triumphantly. She pointed to a low bush heavy with elderberries and began picking. Jae-Mi quickly joined her.

"Su-Na!" Jae-Mi called. "Aren't you going to help?"

"It isn't fair for us to do all the work," Hi-Jong replied.

When the two sisters looked up, they could see that Su-Na wasn't anywhere nearby. Where had she gone? "Go find her," Jai-Mi said. "She's probably farther up the path. We haven't much light left."

Hi-Jong and Jae-Mi hurried along and found Su-

Na sitting under a twisted pine tree that towered over-head. Perched on a rock, she was busy scribbling something on a piece of paper. "Su-Na!" Hi-Jong said.

Her sister looked up, startled. She jammed the paper into her pocket.

"What are you doing?" Jae-Mi demanded. "Come and help us."

"Just looking at the view," Su-Na said. She sighed and leaned back against the tree. "This is such a peaceful place. You can forget all your troubles here."

Hi-Jong frowned. "And you can also forget about your promises, too."

"You said you'd help us," Jae-Mi whined. "Come on! We need you."

"First come and take a look," Su-Na insisted. She helped her sisters up on the rock so that they could look out on the mountains that stretched into the dis-tance. Already the purple shadows were changing and deepening as light from the setting sun began to shift.

Hi-Jong looked up into the great dark branches of the pine tree and felt very safe. "It is peaceful. I don't think anything bad could ever happen here."

Su-Na laughed. "Strong *nun-chi'i*. That's what Grandmother would say. She believed all trees and rocks had special spirits."

"I don't remember her," Hi-Jong said.

"When Father asks, I pretend I do so I don't hurt his feelings," Jae-Mi admitted. "I don't remember anything about Korea anymore except what other people told me. It's all mixed-up memories. What do you remember?"

Su-Na picked a fresh twig and held it to her nose like a mustache. "I remember a few things. Grandfather's scratchy face." She laughed. "I remember sweet, stringy *yut* candy from Grandfather's pocket and Grandmother crawling way up in the roof beams to place pine bows to appease the spirits of the kitchen and the *kimchee* jar. I was so worried she'd fall. 'Come down, Grandmother!' I shouted."

Hi-Jong giggled. "What else?"

"Being carried on someone's back." Su-Na paused and frowned. "Soldiers' boots. I remember when the Japanese soldiers came and we had to leave very quickly and everyone was upset. I wasn't upset. I thought it was exciting to go on a trip. I didn't know we'd be going away for such a long time."

"Someday we'll go back. Father said," Hi-Jong said quietly. "But I am tired of moving. Are you?"

Su-Na nodded. She looked quickly away so that her sisters could not see her face. "Let's come back here and decorate this tree with cloth and pieces of ribbon and paper to please the spirits. That will make this a special *nun-chi'i* place."

Hi-Jong and Jae-Mi agreed that that was a very good idea.

"It will be our secret place," Jae-Mi said. She loved secrets.

When they finally returned home with a basket only half full of berries, Mother's face was very worried. "It's dark. Where were you? You should never be out so late like this in the mountains. It isn't safe. There are rattlesnakes, tarantula spiders—"

"We found beautiful berries," Hi-Jong said. "See?"

Jae-Mi winked at Su-Na.

"Hurry and eat your dinner now," Mother said in a distracted voice. "I need help with the laundry. You neglect your chores."

"Sorry, Mother," Su-Na said. "And where is Father? Won't he be pleased to see the wild fruit?"

"He's sleeping."

"So early?" Su-Na asked.

"Do not wake him," Mother replied. She brushed a strand of hair from her face. "Now go."

The next day at school was the very best kind of all because it rained. The rain came down in sheets and torrents. It drummed against the roof and rattled against the chimney pipe. Su-Na and her sisters were delighted it was raining because that meant that the Mexican children's mothers would come bringing tortillas to warm on the stove. And Miss V would heat a can of mysterious Campbell Soup. Su-Na had never seen anything so incredible before. And once, she had felt very privileged when Miss V let her taste a spoonful. It was very good even though it came out of a can. Every time it rained they had an indoor picnic. And because the Mexican mothers were always very generous, they let Su-Na and her sisters have a tortilla, too. The sisters loved to eat the flat white corn meal pancake with spicy beans rolled up inside.

Best of all for Su-Na was that on the days they had the tortilla picnics Ramon came. He was nearly seventeen and he did not go to school anymore, but he helped his mother carry the large basket filled with tortillas. The same way he carried the wood to the school house for his father. Su-Na admired how helpful and considerate and strong he was. What she admired most of all were his beautiful dark eyes.

She never spoke to him, even today when he came in the schoolhouse and Miss V was sitting at her desk writing something in the big book with everyone's names. The minute Su-Na saw Ramon, she thought she could not breathe. How could she talk? She had no air in her lungs. It had all escaped and she felt dizzy, as if she had run all the way up a mountain without stopping.

The schoolhouse echoed with happy voices. "Tortilla?" one of the mothers called. The children shot up their hands to ask for more.

Hi-Jong had found a nice warm spot in the corner where she sat with Yuki, her best friend in the class. Yuki was a year younger than Hi-Jong. Like Hi-Jong, she enjoyed baking mud cakes with acorn decorations, fashioning dancing shoes from leaves, and creating small fairy castles with twigs an

Hi-Jong's sisters did not have the pat

interest in such activities, she truly appre

company. "We are soul sisters," she once

Yuki, who nodded solemnly.

"Do you know Yuki is Japanese?" Jae-Mi once whispered to her sister in a low warning voice.

"So?" Hi-Jong replied. "There are no other Koreans here. Why does it matter? She is my friend." She said her words in an even way, pronouncing each one as if it meant something else. Something that Jae-Mi could never misunderstand. What she meant to imply, of course, was "And you will never mention it to Mother or Father." Neither of them wanted to experience their parents' wrath or hear yet again Father's stay-with-your-own-kind speech. Hi-Jong knew that Jae-Mi would never tattle or endanger her friendship after what had happened to Kyoko. Never.

What increasingly confounded Jae-Mi and Hi-Jong was Su-Na. Every day she seemed to become stranger and stranger. At first they thought it was because she studied too much. She read too much. She wrote too much. One day, however, when they were supposed to be delivering laundry, they finally noticed how Su-Na insisted on walking down a street next to houses where there were no deliveries.

"What are we doing here?" Jae-Mi demanded, huffing and puffing.

 'I thought this would be a nice way to walk," Su-Na replied. She kept looking around as if the area were scenic.

Hi-Jong inspected the few ramshackle miners' cabins clinging to the hillside. There was nothing nice about these houses. Was her sister crazy? "You are making our delivery route much longer," she complained.

And suddenly, without warning, someone came down the steps of one of the ramshackle houses. He was the same boy they had seen in the schoolhouse while they waited on the step, the same boy they had seen at all the tortilla picnics. Only this time his dark, wavy hair was combed as if with water so that the comb marks still showed. And he was wearing a clean shirt. He was smiling directly at Su-Na.

Su-Na's hand went up in a ridiculous fluttering greeting. She acted as if she did not even remember that her sisters were watching her.

Hi-Jong and Jae-Mi exchanged glances. Now they understood. For a split second Jae-Mi considered what to say to her older sister. Should she tell her? Didn't she know already? Cautiously, Jae-Mi cleared her throat and said in her wisest sisterly voice, "He's not Korean."

Su-Na turned. Her face glowed with happiness. She looked almost beautiful. "I know," she replied as if Jae-Mi's observation was the most ridiculous thing she had ever heard in her life.

Chapter 13

What is love like?
Is it round or is it square?
Long or short? Is there more
To measure than what I'm stepping on?
You may not think it lasts long
But I can't see where it ends.

"Meung is sick," Mother said as soon as the girls returned from delivering the laundry. Her voice was frantic. She pointed toward the bedroom. "I have to go to the grocery store for a moment. Will you watch the boys?" Mother placed plump one-and-a-half-year-old Edward into Hi-Jong's lap. Then Mother took a chair and climbed to a high shelf. She pulled down a battered tobacco tin and pried it open with great effort. Carefully, she counted out some coins.

"Isn't that Grandmother's *hwangap* money?" Su-Na asked.

"Go!" Mother shouted when she noticed Su-Na and Hi-Jong watching her. "I gave you a job. Watch your brothers."

Su-Na and Hi-Jong scurried to the room where Jae-Mi was already hovering over their three-year-old brother. He was carefully covered with the best coverlet. "What's wrong, little dragon?" Hi-Jong called.

Meung did not smile. His eyes looked very dark and large.

"Do you have a fever?" Su-Na asked. She placed a hand on his smooth forehead. His forehead was very hot. "If he has a pain in the stomach, we could try rubbing his stomach with a cat's skin. We could get him some *insam*. That's what they call ginseng in Korea. Very powerful but very expensive. Meung, let me hear you cough," Su-Na commanded. Her brother obeyed.

"Doesn't sound like a donkey-cough," Su-Na said. "If you had a donkey-cough we'd have to give you medicine made from donkey hair to get out the bad spirit that's tickling your throat. I hope it's not smallpox."

"He looks bad," Hi-Jong agreed. She sat down on his pallet. After listening to his sisters, Meung looked more distressed than ever.

"I know what he needs," Jae-Mi said to her sisters in a confidential tone. "He told me. He needs canned peaches."

"Canned peaches?" Su-Na said. Canned peaches were very costly. In her entire life, she had only had them once. And she could still remember how sweet and tender they tasted. "I'm afraid we cannot afford such an extravagance."

"He says he will die without them," Jae-Mi said sadly.

"I need them," Meung said.

"What if canned peaches are the only thing that will make him well?" Hi-Jong asked. "It would be terrible if he died."

Su-Na studied their precious brother and pondered this question for a moment. Was it possible to die from not having something you wanted more than anything in the world? In her own life she could think of one person who would cause her such an emotion, such a terrible longing. Was love for a person the same as the absolute need for canned peaches?

"What should we do?" Jae-Mi asked.

Hi-Jong took a deep breath. "Does Mother know?"

Meung nodded slowly as if moving his head caused him great pain. "Perhaps that's why she went to the grocery," Su-Na said. "We'll have to wait a little longer till she comes back."

Meung was so distraught about having to wait that he began to whimper and cry in a most pathetic *nun-mul* manner. "There, there," said Hi-Jong, who was always sympathetic when someone else sobbed.

By the time Mother returned, Meung was nearly beside himself. "He's burning up," Su-Na said. "It's a good thing you're back. Did you find them?"

"What?" Mother said as she frantically checked Meung's forehead.

"The canned peaches," Su-Na replied.

Mother shook her head. "There were none at the store. The closest other grocery is over in Great Bear, two miles away. It's too late to go now. The store's closed. Besides, it is dark and dangerous on the road."

Meung began to sob again. His shoulders shook.

"I could go in the morning," Su-Na promised.

"You will miss school," Jae-Mi said. "Let me go." Jae-Mi would gladly go and skip school for once. Going to Great Bear in the sunlight on a fine day when everyone else was trapped indoors at school sounded like fun to her.

Finally, after a small amount of coaxing, Mother agreed to send both Su-Na and her sisters first thing in the morning. Somehow Meung managed to make it through the night. The next morning, before Father went to work, the three sisters hurried off with a handkerchief filled with precious coins.

The sun had not even risen over the mountains. The valleys were filled with cool, damp mist but the girls hurried bravely on. They followed the path through the forest. An owl flapped in one of the trees, sending down a shower of raindrops clinging to the pine needles. Nearby came the sound of water rushing. A sudden rise in the river had washed away the original crude bridge a few weeks earlier. Three rough logs had been placed side by side to form a temporary walkway across the deep water. The girls edged their way across the logs. They tried not to look down into the water until they got close enough to the opposite side to leap safely to shore.

Finally they reached Great Bear. Su-Na and her sisters walked quickly down the dirt road that was the main street of the little mining town and knocked at the door of the grocery store. There were a few people on the street, mostly coming out of the three saloons.

No one answered their knock.

Hi-Jong pounded as hard as she could. "What if they don't answer?"

Finally, they heard someone cursing on the other side of the door. The bolt latch slid open. The door swung wide. "What do you want so early?" the storekeeper muttered.

"Canned peaches," Su-Na said. "Our brother is dying."

The storekeeper yawned. He pulled his suspenders up over his shoulder and signaled for the girls to come inside. The store was very dark and smelled of cats and musty cheese. "You got money?"

"Yes, sir," Su-Na said. She held up the handkerchief and counted out the coins. There was just enough for one can. She paid for the peaches and the sisters retraced their steps back to Idria.

On the way across the log footbridge Su-Na held the can tight against herself. At the middle of the bridge, she heard Jae-Mi call, "Su-Na! Su-Na, look —"

Startled, Su-Na lost her grip. *Splash!*

The canned peaches sank like a rock. Hi-Jong screamed. Su-Na stood there, stunned. She stared at the spot where the can had disappeared in the current. The swift, cold water had to be at least four feet deep. They would never get it out. None of them could swim. What would Mother say? Their money was gone and Meung was going to die. It was all her fault.

"Su-Na!" Jae-Mi called, insistent this time.

Su-Na looked up. Standing at the end of the bridge was Ramon. He had something slung over his shoulder. A large bag. Su-Na stared at him as if she did not know who he was. She felt completely foolish. "I . . . I . . ." she began and stopped.

"She dropped the can in the water. We need it. We have no more money. Our brother is dying," Jae-Mi said quickly. "Can you get it for us?" She pointed to the spot in the water where the can had disappeared.

Ramon did not say anything. In spite of the cold, he slipped off his shoes, his shirt, and plunged into the water. When he came up, he did not have the can. He plunged again.

The girls knew the river was very cold. How could

he stand it? They waited, terrified he would drown or freeze to death. This time when he came up he held a rock.

He plunged again.

Su-Na prayed he would not drown. She waited and waited.

When he finally came up, he held the gleaming can. He splashed up onto the rocks, shivering and dripping with water. He handed Su-Na the can. She could not decide which was more beautiful, the gleaming can or heroic Ramon. *"Gracias,"* she murmured.

He smiled at her, put his shirt back on, and slipped on his shoes. Then he flung the bag over his shoulder and disappeared down the trail.

"You know Spanish?" Hi-Jong arched one eyebrow.

"A little," Su-Na replied. She walked quickly ahead of her sisters. "Come on. Let's hurry."

When they arrived home, Mother did not seem to notice that the can's label was mostly soggy and torn. She opened the can and fed the peaches to Meung. He was delighted and smiled for the first time in three days.

"You should have seen who we saw on our way home," Jae-Mi said mischievously as she watched Mother feed Meung the last of the peaches.

"Who?" Mother asked.

Su-Na shot her sister a threatening glance.

"The old burro who used to live up the road," Jae-Mi replied, and smiled at Su-Na.

Meung quickly recovered. Of all his sisters, Su-Na was the most convinced that the peaches had sped up his recovery.

Weeks passed. One Saturday afternoon in late winter when the mine was closed for a short holiday, Father announced that he was sad to see the old ways of Korea being lost and forgotten by his family. Su-Na looked up from the book she was reading. Jae-Mi and Hi-Jong, who were busy cutting out pictures from a catalog, didn't hear what Father said. Their two brothers, rolling around on the floor of the kitchen, did not know what Father was talking about.

"I am going to give you lessons myself," he said. He spread a folded piece of newspaper on the table. "I am going to teach you the alphabet."

"Father," Hi-Jong said in a bored voice, "we know the alphabet."

"I am teaching the Korean alphabet," Father said. "Come here and see what I write."

With the stub of a pencil, he drew some *hangul* script. "These are the letters used to read Korean. You must try to make the characters fit inside a square. Surely you remember them, Su-Na? My own mother taught them to you."

Su-Na studied the characters carefully. A few looked familiar. She tried to copy them. "Too sprawled! Too lopsided!" Father criticized. "Don't squeeze the pencil so tight." He sighed with disappointment when it was clear that Su-Na had forgotten almost everything. "Too American!" he said, and shook his head.

"Father, you said you wanted us to be American. So we are American. Now you say, be Korean. How can we be two things at once?" Jae-Mi demanded impatiently.

"Ai-goo! This is what I am talking about. Disrespect. In Korea you would never talk to your elder in such a way," Father said angrily. He looked at Mother. She was watching what was happening from the ironing table. Her mouth was closed tight.

" 'Obedience to one's parents is the mother of one hundred virtues,' " Father said.

Su-Na bowed in agreement. "That is true," she said slowly. She did not wish to enrage her father. The last time she had gotten into an argument with him, he began coughing so badly he had to go to bed. "Father, you must understand it is not like Korea in America. There are many different kinds of people here. We have to get along. You said that yourself, remember?"

Father threw the pencil on the table in disgust. "Some things are never different. Just because we are surrounded by different people doesn't mean we act like them. We don't believe what they believe. They cannot be our friends."

"Then how will we ever understand each other?" Su-Na asked.

"You are a difficult girl," Father said angrily. "You

used to listen politely and be silent. Now you speak too much. It is that school. That American schoolteacher."

Su-Na bit her lip. "I like Miss V. She says if I pass a test I can go to high school someday."

"And your brothers? What about them? High school is expensive. We need to save money for them."

"I can earn my own way," Su-Na said quietly. This was not the way she had planned to have this conversation. She wanted to ask her parents when they were happy — not angry. Everything was falling apart.

"I'm sorry, no, it's out of the question. No high school for you. We need all the money you will earn," Father said. He sat down on the chair and began coughing. He held his sides.

"Su-Na!" Mother said angrily. "Now see what you have done." She hurried to Father and poured a tin cup with water. Then she dipped a rag in water and held it to the back of his neck.

Su-Na ran from the house. She rushed into the darkness and walked a very long way before she realized that there was snow on the ground and her arms were covered with white.

For many days afterward, Father refused to speak to Su-Na. She refused to speak to him. Life in the little house became very awkward and tense.

Fortunately, spring came early that year. A warm chinook blew in from the Pacific one morning and by afternoon all the snow in the mountains had begun to melt. Pale blue bell-shaped flowers, the first to appear in the spring, began blooming in the sheltered places on the south side of boulders and among the trees. One day Jae-Mi came home and discovered on the table a small glass jelly jar filled with the first delicate wild flowers. Immediately, she knew who these were for and who they were from.

"Father," Jae-Mi said when she came home with her sisters from school, "look at these."

Su-Na gave her sister a meaningful glance, then looked away in embarrassment.

"They are for you, Father," Jae-Mi continued. "From Su-Na, begging your forgiveness."

Father took the flowers and smelled them. He seemed very pleased. "Thank you, little pigeon," he said. "You are forgiven."

Su-Na made a graceful bow. She watched, stunned, as her father walked away carrying the bouquet that had been given to her by Ramon. Jae-Mi, who enjoyed secrets more than anything, winked at her sister playfully.

School ended a few months later. Summer returned and Su-Na vanished whenever she could into the mountains. Her sisters felt neglected and wondered why she always looked so happy when she returned. Was it because of the power of the *nun-chi'i* tree?

Their second year in school passed quickly. Su-Na

studied hard when she wasn't working at the school-house or for Mother. "Your nose is always in a book," Jae-Mi complained. "You have no time for us."

Su-Na did not answer. She seldom spoke to her sisters. She spoke even less to Father. Su-Na and Father seemed to pass each other in the house like hostile ghosts.

To escape their family's growing unpleasantness, Jae-Mi and Hi-Jong depended more and more on each other. When they finished their chores, they played outdoors as much as they could. Sometimes they built castles with tree branches in the forest. Sometimes they piled rocks in the stream to make dams for their new kingdoms' trout pools and swimming beaches. Not even exhausted Mother seemed to notice the girls' absence. She was too tired or preoccupied with the demands of their boisterous, whining brothers.

In August 1910 a small graduation party was planned for the students leaving the school in Idria. There were only three people who had finished the eighth grade. One of them was Su-Na. She was sixteen and looked very pretty in the white dress with a blue sash that her mother had carefully pressed. Mother helped braid and pin up her hair. Su-Na felt delighted for once to be treated like a grown-up.

In just a week she secretly planned to take the test for high school. Miss V had sent away for all the necessary papers. Su-Na wanted to tell Mother, but she couldn't. Not yet. "You are the brightest student I have ever had," Miss V had proudly told Su-Na. "I have great hopes for you."

Su-Na did not want to disappoint her.

Just as Su-Na, her sisters, brothers, and mother were about to leave for the schoolhouse, Father staggered in from work. His face was dirty and he looked shaken. "What is it?" Mother demanded. "Are you hurt? Did you lose your job? Why are you home so early?"

Su-Na glanced nervously at the clock. The graduation ceremony would start soon.

Father sat on a bench and placed a Korean newspaper on the table. Slowly, he opened it and pointed to an article on the front page. Since neither Su-Na nor her sisters could read Korean, they waited for Father to read aloud. He rubbed his eyes. His voice sounded dead. "We are *yumin* now."

"Drifting people?" Mother asked. She sat down, too. "So it has happened."

"What? What has happened?" Jae-Mi demanded. She shoved Meung with his sticky fingers away from her clean skirt.

"The Japanese have taken over," Father said. "There is no more Korea. The Japanese have changed the laws, the language, the government. Everything. We have no country to go back to. Our country is gone."

Mother looked stunned. She leaned forward and wept softly.

Su-Na cleared her throat. Her sisters, too, looked anxious. "Can we go now, please?" Su-Na said in a careful voice.

Mother dabbed her eyes with her sleeve. "The graduation. I nearly forgot." She started to stand up.

Father stopped her. "We are going nowhere," he said in a monotone voice. "Nowhere."

Mother sat down again. She glanced beseechingly at Su-Na as if to say, *Be patient. Be quiet for once.*

"Nowhere, Father?" Su-Na asked. "But what about the ceremony? I have worked so hard for this day. I have —"

"Silence!" Father shouted. He crumpled the newspaper in his two fists. Before he could jump to his feet, Su-Na hurried across the room, kicked open the door, and fled the house.

Chapter

14

What shall I be
When I am dead?
The tallest pine tree
On the highest peak.
When snow covers the world,
I will still be green.

In late October a rumor spread quickly through Idria that something wonderful was coming, something no one had ever seen before. A silent picture show. "It is free," Jae-Mi told Mother when she came home after school with Hi-Jong. "Many different pictures moving just like real life."

"What can this be?" Mother said. She folded piles of laundry that she had taken from the line.

"They are going to show it in town on the side of a

185

building tonight," Hi-Jong said. "Can we go, please? Can we go?"

Mother frowned. There were still three more deliveries to be made that afternoon. Since Su-Na was working in the boardinghouse in town as a cook, she could not help at home the way she once did. Mother had to depend on her two youngest daughters to make the deliveries and help take care of the two little ones. "I don't know," Mother said. "What does your father say?"

Hi-Jong and Jae-Mi looked at each other nervously. "We have not asked him," replied Hi-Jong, who knew better than to try to speak directly about anything possibly controversial with their father these days. He was still bitter and resentful about what was happening in Korea. Unfortunately, he seemed to be taking his frustrations out on Su-Na.

Their eldest sister had become sullen and secretive since school started. Hi-Jong and her sister could not understand why Su-Na was acting so resentful about taking a job in town. What was so terrible about not going to high school?

"Mother, we want to do something fun," Jae-Mi complained. "Everyone is so gloomy around here. Please let us go."

Mother sighed. "You may go, if you take Meung with you."

"What about Su-Na?" Hi-Jong complained.

"She may go, too, I suppose," Mother said in a distracted voice. "You must come home immediately when the show ends. Do not speak to anyone."

Jae-Mi sighed. Her parents were so strict and old-fashioned. She did not want to be bossed around by gloomy Su-Na. Hi-Jong, too, was disappointed. Now they'd have to take bratty five-year-old Meung. She was looking forward to going to the picture show with Yuki. What if Meung told Father about Yuki? They would only have to hope that Meung would not notice she was Japanese and would not say anything when they got home.

That evening when it became dark, Jae-Mi and Hi-Jong took their brother to town, where they hoped to meet Yuki. Su-Na walked with them. She was wearing a pretty, clean dress with a bright blue sash and a matching ribbon in her hair. "You're awfully quiet," Jae-Mi said to her distracted eldest sister.

"Must I always talk? I have things on my mind," Su-Na replied in a very grown-up, impatient voice. She looked around expectantly as they walked into town.

"Unpleasant as usual," Hi-Jong whispered to Jae-Mi. "Let's not sit with her."

But before they could escape from Su-Na, she escaped from them. The next moment that Hi-Jong looked around, Su-Na had disappeared into the crowd.

"Look at all the people!" Jae-Mi said. Someone had set up a stand to sell refreshments. There were chairs and benches lined up outside of the dry goods store. The picture show was going to be shown on the side of the building. Hi-Jong waved when she saw Yuki in the crowd. Yuki had generously brought sweet rice cakes her mother made as a treat.

"Who's this?" Yuki asked.

Meung smiled in a charming manner and held out his pudgy hand for a rice cake. "Our brother," Jae-Mi replied unhappily. "Don't pay any attention to him. We had to bring him along. Sorry."

"Here," Yuki said and gave him a rice cake. "He certainly likes to eat."

The girls found four seats together in the front row. The crowd hooted. Suddenly a light flickered on the building. A locomotive charged toward them. Someone screamed. Hi-Jong covered her eyes. Closer and closer the engine roared and then at the last minute veered away. The crowd cheered.

Cowboys on horseback galloped on the screen next. They dashed along beside the train. They waved their arms and shouted but no words came out of their mouths. In the background were mountains that reminded Hi-Jong of the peaks near Idria. The sight seemed so familiar, Hi-Jong glanced up at the dark peaks in the distance. At that moment she caught sight of Su-Na. Her sister looked briefly at her, silent as a deer, then vanished into the crowd.

Where is she going? Hi-Jong thought. But only for a moment. Her attention was focused on the cowboys and the prancing horses. Now they galloped into town. The silent picture changed. Three Chinese men in ancient costumes tottered down the street. The cowboys dramatically jumped off their horses. In bold letters, one word appeared on the screen: "Dance!" The cowboys moved their mouths but no sound came out. They pulled their guns out of their holsters and shot them at the ground. Dust flew. The poor Chinese men began to leap. "Dance!" the screen proclaimed.

The audience howled and clapped its approval. Meung demanded another rice cake from Yuki. He munched and watched as if hypnotized. But Hi-Jong and Jae-Mi felt as if they were shrinking. Yuki, too, slunk down in her seat. Hi-Jong squirmed. *This is horrible.* Jae-Mi nervously looked around at the laughing, jeering faces. The audience clapped louder and louder as the Chinese men danced faster and faster. Meung never took his eyes from the screen.

Hi-Jong tugged on her sister's sleeve. "Let's get out of here," she whispered and signaled to Yuki. "Come on, Meung."

"No," he protested loudly, "I want to stay."

"We're leaving," Jae-Mi said between clenched teeth. She grabbed her brother and hauled him out of his seat. He yowled loudly.

A group of boys sitting behind them instantly took notice. They picked up pebbles and began pelting

Meung, his sisters, and Yuki. "Dance!" the boys shouted gleefully. "Dance!"

Terrified, Meung and the girls rushed away. As fast as they could, they ran down the street toward home. Finally, when they were far enough away from Idria not to hear the crowd anymore, they paused to catch their breath. Yuki began to whimper in the darkness. "We will always be strangers here," she said, gulping. "I'm going home." Her footsteps skittered across the gravel.

"Good-bye," Jae-Mi called, filled with disappointment.

"Come on," Hi-Jong said, and took Meung roughly by the hand. She wished that she could blame him for the disastrous evening, even though she knew deep down it wasn't his fault. "Don't say anything about what happened, Meung, or we will never take you anywhere again."

Meung nodded miserably, uncertain what exactly he had done to cause his sister to be so angry.

When they returned to the house, they noticed the door was opened slightly. They tiptoed closer. Someone inside was crying. Hi-Jong and Jae-Mi froze. They held Meung's hand tight. Now what had happened? The girls pushed open the door and saw Mother sitting at the table, her face in her hands. Father sat beside her with his back toward the door.

At first none of the children could speak, they were so stunned. They had never seen their mother cry this hysterically before. Hi-Jong pushed the door open farther, unsure what to do. Three-year-old Edward was playing on the floor. He was all right. "What is wrong?" she said in a low voice, searching the room for some clue.

"Your sister," Father growled. He turned. His face was angry, dark, and mournful.

"Su-Na has run away. She has disgraced us." Mother wiped her eyes. When had her mouth become such a hard, brittle line?

Jae-Mi and Hi-Jong stared at each other in shock. They could not believe what they heard. *Run away?*

"Where did she go?" Meung asked as if at any moment she'd be back.

"Hush," Jae-Mi said and motioned with her finger for her brother to be quiet. Mother handed Hi-Jong a note written in English. It was in Su-Na's handwriting:

I know you won't approve. I am sixteen. I have a right to some kind of happiness. I am running away to be married to Ramon. I will never return.

"Never?" Hi-Jong said. Guilt choked her throat. She had seen Su-Na in the crowd. She could have stopped her.

"She is dead. She is worse than dead," Mother said in a dull, angry voice. "She is nothing. She is a nonperson."

"Do not speak your sister's name again," Father warned.

Jae-Mi stared at her parents in amazement. How was it that they had become so shriveled and she never noticed? Father's face was ravaged and gaunt. His once proud back was now bent, his handsome face mottled and lined, his hair speckled with white. Mother, too, seemed as shrunken as a bitter, old apple. When had this happened? Why hadn't she noticed before?

Hi-Jong, Jae-Mi, and Meung crept away to their own bedrooms. They lay on the pallets and stared up at the darkness of the ceiling and wondered where Su-Na was. Hi-Jong thought, *Is she safe? Is she happy?* She still loved Su-Na, yet she did not know what to do. "Never see her again?" Hi-Jong whispered to her sister. "Why does it have to be this way?"

Jae-Mi felt a great suffocating sadness envelop her, too. She knew they both still loved their sister even if she had gone away and married someone who was not Korean without Mother or Father's permission. *Obedience to one's parents is the mother of one hundred virtues.* They were obligated to obey their parents, no matter what. "Go to sleep," Jae-Mi hissed. She turned away, her face toward the wall, so that her sister could not hear her hopeless *nun-mul.*

Days passed. The first snow fell. Mysteriously, one by one, Su-Na's scant belongings began to disappear. Her extra shoes. Her too-small dress. Her blanket.

One afternoon Hi-Jong found Father burning a bunch of papers in the rubbish heap. He poked them with a stick. Gray, shriveled ash flew up and floated away.

"Father?" Hi-Jong called.

He turned away from her and wiped his eyes with the back of his hand.

"I must speak with you. Once you told us anything new and strange causes some fear at first. You said ridicule and violence often result. And you talked about fear and ignorance. Do you remember, Father? You also talked about forgiveness." She paused and took a deep breath. "What you and Mother are doing to our sister is not right."

"Do not preach to me," Father said gruffly. "Have you not forgotten that I am your venerable parent? Have you forgotten your place?"

"This is not right. You say one thing but you do something else. How are you so different from the prejudiced white people who despise us?"

Father did not answer. His back stiffened. A muscle in his jaw quivered. Although he could not see her, Hi-Jong bowed briefly and left. She knew she had reached a dangerous boundary. To cross any farther would mean that she, too, would become a nonperson. She had seen what happened to Su-Na and she knew she could not risk the same terrible rejection.

Hi-Jong left the yard and kept walking. She did

not know where she was going, only that she was moving away from her sorrowful home. She walked and walked up into the mountains to escape the smell of smoke and the sound of sadness. She was surprised to hear Jae-Mi's shrill voice calling her. Pausing, she waited for her sister to join her.

The wind moved in the pine trees. The sky was clear and bright. Up here, away from all the people in their lives, their troubles seemed far away. The girls walked along in silence, both knowing why they had come, not knowing where they were headed. "Being different will never go away, no matter how we try to be American," Jae-Mi said in a quiet voice. "We will always be strangers here."

Hi-Jong sighed. "Perhaps we will have to find our own way."

Jae-Mi looked at her younger sister and felt surprise. She had never considered that she could be so wise. Her sister's words gave her an idea. "I know what we should do."

"What?"

"The tree."

The girls hurried to the place that Su-Na loved so much high on the mountainside. They stripped from the pine tree's branches the old, dead flowers and attached new sprigs of berries and looped bows made from long, dried grass. They each untied one lace from their boot and made more bows.

"Do you think Su-Na will come here and see this?" Jae-Mi asked.

Hi-Jong shrugged. "The tree has powerful *nun-chi'i*." They waited a long time under the pine that bent and shivered in the wind. When it became too dark, they went home.

For three evenings in a row they returned, each time smuggling a bit of ribbon, some colorful strips of paper, pieces of material snipped from their sashes. If anyone noticed, they would get in trouble for this, but they did not care.

Each time they returned, they hoped for some sign that Su-Na had been there and seen what they had made for her. Not until the fourth evening did they sense that something had changed.

Dangling from the tree branch was the bright blue sash from Su-Na's best dress. Wrapped tightly inside a knot was a piece of lined paper folded like a star. Hi-Jong unfolded the paper with trembling hands and read aloud:

"We are living in Willows. I am well and fine. We work on a farm. Someday we will have our own. We will be American. Do not forget me. Always I will find a way to reach you or you will reach me.

—Poksili"

Hi-Jong and Jae-Mi felt tremendous joy. They read and reread the note. It was like talking to someone they had feared was dead and gone forever. What was even more amazing was that Su-Na had signed the note with a nickname she was given as a baby. *Poksili.* The nickname meant Happy. More than anything, this gave them the greatest hope of all.

"We will find a way," Hi-Jong said. "We will never be parted."

Jae-Mi nodded. "No matter what happens, we will always be sisters."

Bibliography

Asian Women United of California, ed. *Making Waves.* Boston: Beacon Press, 1989.

Baron, Virginia Olsen, ed. *Sunset in a Spider Web: Sijo Poetry of Ancient Korea.* NY: Holt, Rinehart and Winston, 1974.

Bode, Janet. *New Kids on the Block: Oral Histories of Immigrant Teens.* NY: Franklin Watts, 1989.

Carpenter, Frances. *Tales of a Korean Grandmother.* Garden City, NY: 1947.

Chan, Sucheng. *Asian Americans.* Boston: Tayne Publishers, 1991.

Charr, Easurk Emsen. *The Golden Mountain: Autobiography of a Korean Immigrant, 1895-1960.* Chicago: University of Illinois Press, 1961.

Chow, Claire S. *Leaving Deep Water: The Lives of Asian*

American Women at the Crossroads of Two Cultures. NY: Dutton, 1998.

Choy, Bong-youn. *Koreans in America.* Chicago: Nelson-Hall, 1979.

Farkas, Lani Ah Tye. *Bury My Bones in America.* Nevada City: Carl Mautz Publishing, 1998.

Hoare, James and Pares, Susan. *Korea.* NY: Kegan Paul International, 1988.

Hongo, Garrett, ed. *Under Western Eyes.* NY: Anchor Books/Doubleday, 1995.

Howe, Russell Warren. *The Koreans: Passion and Grace.* NY: Harcourt Brace Jovanovich, 1988.

Jewett, Eleanore M. *Which Was Witch? Tales of Ghosts and Magic from Korea.* NY: Viking Press, 1953.

Lee, Ki-Baik. *A New History of Korea.* Seoul, Korea: Ilchokak Publishers, 1984.

Lee, Mary Paik. *Quiet Odyssey: A Pioneer Korean Woman in America.* Seattle: University of Washington Press, 1990.

Oliver, Robert T. *A History of the Korean People in Modern Times.* Newark: University of Delaware Press, 1993.

Patterson, Wayne. *The Ilse: First-Generation Immigrants in Hawai'i.* Honolulu: University of Hawaii Press, 2000.

Patterson, Wayne. *The Korean Frontier in America: Immigration to Hawaii, 1896–1910.* Honolulu: University of Hawaii Press, 1988.

Robertson, Susan L., ed. *Women, America, and Movement: Narratives of Relocation.* Columbia, MO: University of Missouri Press, 1998.

Takaki, Ronald. *Strangers from a Different Shore: A History of Asian Americans.* NY: Penguin Books, 1989.

Yu, Diana. *Winds of Change.* Silver Spring, MD: The Women's Institute Press, 1991.

About the Author

Trained as a journalist, Laurie Lawlor worked for many years as a freelance writer and editor before devoting herself full-time to the creation of children's books. She enjoys many speaking engagements at schools and libraries, and her books have been nominated for many awards. She lives in Evanston, Illinois, with her husband, son, daughter, and two large Labrador retrievers. Her books include the *Addie Across the Prairie* series, the *Heartland* series, *How to Survive Third Grade*, *The Worm Club*, *Gold in the Hills*, and *Little Women* (a movie novelization). Her nonfiction work, *Shadow Catcher: The Life and Work of Edward S. Curtis*, won the Carl Sandburg Award for nonfiction (1995) and the Golden Kite Honor Book Award (1995).